THE
DARK
BLUE
100-
RIDE
BUS TICKET

W0007122

THE DARK BLUE 100-RIDE BUS TICKET

MARGARET MAHY

HarperCollins*Publishers*

National Library of New Zealand Cataloguing-in-Publication Data
Mahy, Margaret.
Dark blue hundred-ride bus ticket / Margaret Mahy.
ISBN 978-1-86950-816-6
[1. Fantasy. 2. Courage—Fiction. 3. Supermarkets—Fiction.]
I. Title.
NZ823.2—dc 22

First published 2009
HarperCollins*Publishers (New Zealand) Limited*
PO Box 1, Shortland Street, Auckland 1140

ISBN 978 1 86950 816 6

Cover design by Natalie Winter
Cover images by Shutterstock.com
Typesetting by Springfield West

Printed by Griffin Press, Australia

50gsm Bulky News used by HarperCollins*Publishers* is a natural,
recyclable product made from wood grown in sustainable
plantation forests. The manufacturing processes conform to the
environmental regulations in the country of origin, New Zealand.

chapter one

THE DARK BLUE
HUNDRED-RIDE BUS TICKET

When Carlo came out of hospital he had to stay in bed at the new flat he shared with his mother, Jessica, and, though it was new (well, new to them) he quickly became very tired of it. He grew tired of its brownness and its sad, dusty smell, and tired of the little, squashed-up windows, which all looked out onto the grey concrete wall of the building next door. He didn't even bother to look out of those windows, except by accident. There was nothing to see but grey, which wasn't much better than brown. And it was impossible for Carlo and Jessica to cheer themselves up by playing bright music and singing and dancing. If they made any loud noise — even if they only laughed loudly — their landlady, who lived in the flat above, thumped on the floor with a broom, trying to shut them up. This new-old-brown flat was cheap, of course. That was the good thing about it. They badly needed 'cheap'.

And of course Carlo had no friends here. He'd had to leave his best friend, Harding, behind him when they shifted. He longed for company but no one came to visit him, though Jessica was able to take time off work every now and then. She sat by his bed and read him adventure stories, or helped him to paint pictures with no brown or grey in them. Things could have been a lot worse. But, all the same, it was a day of great rejoicing for them both when the doctor said Carlo was allowed to get up and out into the world again.

'I'm feeling better and better,' he told Jessica, 'but I've been in bed for too long. I wish I had a friend or two next door. And I need a few adventures. Adventures ought to really *happen* to — to someone like me.' Carlo waved his arms around. 'They ought to be out in the air, being free, not shut up in books all the time.'

'Let's be careful,' Jessica said, interrupting him. 'Adventures often happen because something has gone wrong. I'm sorry you haven't got any friends just yet. I know what it's like, because I could do with a good friend or two. But hey — we're so friendly ourselves, I'm sure we'll both find friends sooner or later. Anyhow, let's go off and away to the supermarket. That's a nice, ordinary, outside thing to do.'

Jessica was right. Going to the supermarket was definitely ordinary. Yet on this particular day there turned out to be something unexpected about that ordinary world out there — it wanted to take them by surprise. All the way to the supermarket Carlo saw signs of good luck coming his way. He managed to step over every crack in the pavement — that was the first lucky sign. And then the sun came out just as they were going past a window full of mirrors, and all the mirrors suddenly turned to dazzling silver and signalled to them — that was the second. He found ten cents outside the butcher's shop while his mother was inside buying soup bones and then, just outside the supermarket, he came across Mrs Christmas — the strangest good-luck person he had seen in a long time.

She didn't seem to be much taller than him, and was pulling her supermarket trolley along, growling at it back over her shoulder as if it were a disobedient dog she was trying to take for a walk. Hanging from her wrists were bracelets and bangles; strung around her neck were chains of silver and gold and lots of big, bright glass beads, which reminded Carlo of Christmas tree lights. Indeed, if a Christmas tree had wandered into a supermarket car park and started to pull a trolley around, it would have looked almost exactly like this strange, old woman in her dark green skirt, her two dark green jerseys and her red velvet jacket. Not only that, her hair was dyed dark blue, and she wore a golden star in the front, which glittered beautifully, even though it was tilted over sideways. One star-spike seemed to be tangling in her left eyebrow. Carlo thought someone so Christmassy might actually smell of pine needles, and he slid close behind her, just to have a bit of a sniff.

She stepped back onto him, pinching his toes. He squeaked; she gave a little scream and almost overbalanced. The trolley chuckled to itself and toppled sideways. Groceries tumbled out, scuttling away in every direction, trying to escape. People turned to stare, then moved off quickly, probably anxious to get away from wildly scuttling groceries, or from too much clinking and chiming, or maybe from too much brightness, topped by a tilting star.

'Oh dear,' said the old woman. 'Clumsy of me! Clumsy Katerina Christmas!'

Carlo could *not* believe his ears. Here was a person who not only looked like a Christmas tree, but who was actually called 'Christmas' — it seemed too perfect a match to be true. A moment later he was astonished to see his mother patting Mrs Christmas on the shoulder.

'I'm sorry. It was all our fault, what with Carlo walking so closely behind you. Hey, Carlo! Pick up those things! Oh! Some of your eggs are broken. I'll pay for them.'

Carlo looked at Jessica. They had scarcely enough money to last the week. He would need new sandals when he started school again, and Jessica needed new everything, yet here she was, offering to pay for someone else's broken eggs, and apologizing for an accident that had been nothing to do with her. After all, she had been several steps ahead when he had tried to smell pine needles on the old Christmas-tree of a woman. He began to pick up some of the fallen groceries, but couldn't help telling Jessica off — just a little bit.

'Mum!' he cried. 'We'll run out of money before the end of the week.'

'I know,' said Jessica. 'But this poor lady might be even worse off. Some people are, you know.'

Mrs Christmas was watching and waiting for them. 'Thank you so much,' she said in a hurried, rustling voice that turned everything it said into some sort of secret. 'I was so confused and, between you and me, I really *am* low on cash. It does come and go, doesn't it? And there's always more going than coming. You can't imagine what it's like having to worry about every last cent.' Then she looked at Jessica and Carlo and shrugged her shoulders, jingling her chains and bracelets. 'Well, maybe you do.'

'The supermarkets get so crowded, don't they?' said Jessica. 'Everyone on top of everyone else, all of us looking for "specials".'

'I've never seen anything like it,' said Mrs Christmas. 'Of course, I mostly do my shopping at an entirely different *other* supermarket. I *mostly* go to the Supermarket at the End of the World.'

Jessica laughed. 'It sounds like a long way to go for frozen peas!'

'Oh yes! It *is* a long way off.' Mrs Christmas stood there, jingling and flapping and ballooning in the breeze. 'But the bus service gets you there quickly enough — if you get the right bus. Of course it must be absolutely the right bus. You take Number 13 — the dark BLUE one. It stops wherever you want it to — it's very convenient — but, once it's picked you up, it goes on until it gets to the End of the World, and then it turns around and comes back again. Because, after all, it couldn't go any further than the End of the World, even if someone asked. Otherwise it would drop right over the edge, and no one would want it to do that, even if they happened to have a parachute with them. I mean it's such a long way to fall . . . impossible to climb back, even with spiked boots, so . . . well . . . it stands to reason nobody would enjoy . . . that is to say, the End of the World is . . . and the supermarket . . . that too . . .'

Her sentence was breaking up and going in all directions, behaving in the same disobedient-dog way her supermarket trolley had behaved. She coughed, clearing leftover words out of her throat, and began again, being stern with her sentences this time. 'Look, I'll be leaving town tomorrow . . . my son's coming for me. His wife, who is such a nice girl, has got a job sorting out international rainbows, and they need someone to be at home

11

after school — they've got twenty-seven children, and it keeps them utterly busy — so I'm going to live with them for a bit, baby-sitting, and making a pudding or two, and . . . well . . . there's always feeding the dog — oh and the elephant as well, which is a big job, with elephants eating so much — so what with this and that . . . well, the thing is . . .' This new sentence began escaping from her just as the first one had done, branching out and then dissolving into the open air.

'How lovely,' Jessica said in her most polite, interested voice.

Mrs Christmas caught her own runaway sentence mid-air, and pulled it back again. 'The thing is I won't be *needing* it for quite a while — my hundred-ride ticket, that is — which means it's definitely time for someone else to take my place. After all, we all have to move over some time, don't we? Someone passed it on to me years ago and now it's my job to pass it on again.'

From some pocket under the jacket and jerseys she whisked out a card — a dark blue card, a concession card for a bus — and handed it to Carlo. 'That'll make up for having me stand on your foot.'

'It's really good of you . . .' Jessica began.

But Mrs Christmas smiled, and shook her head so hard she jingled like a money box filled with glass coins. 'Well, as I just told you, someone passed it on to me in the first place,' she said. '*He* decided he was going to live with the unicorns, so . . . what with the this-and-that of things . . . he didn't need bus tickets any more. Unicorns aren't allowed on the bus. They might pierce passengers with their horns, and no bus wants a lot of passenger-piercing — unless people haven't paid for their tickets, of course. Anyhow you'll know when the time comes for *you* to pass it on. You'll recognize the person to give it to, just as I'm recognizing you, but that won't happen for a year or two I don't suppose. Enjoy yourself at the End of the World, but remember to keep away from the edge — oh, and watch out for Dowlers. That's very important. Dowlers are so dangerous. We don't want them dowlerizing the supermarket, do we? Keep your eyes open for their hooves. Now I have to rush, so — bye-bye!'

Before they could ask any questions, off she went, moving very fast for a Christmas tree. Within a minute she had vanished into the crowd, and the sound of her jingling went with her, so they could hear her getting fainter and fainter, even though they couldn't see her any more.

'A bus ticket. What a pretty one,' Jessica said, looking at the ticket in her hand and sounding amused, but a little impressed as well. 'I've never seen one like this before.'

The card was dark blue, powdered with about ninety-five golden stars. There was no doubt about it — it really was a hundred-ride bus ticket. On the top, in golden letters, it said WORLD'S END TRANSPORT SERVICES. Along the bottom it said *Important — keep away from the Edge. Watch out for Dowlers.*

'Good advice, I'm sure,' Jessica said. 'Oh well, we've been out for a while now; time to get you home, I suppose.' She hooked her mostly empty string bag over her arm again, and they began to weave their way back towards the gloomy, brown, sad-smelling flat.

Carlo was feeling thin and pale and already tired, while Jessica wandered along like a mother in a dream. She was so very dreamy she would have missed what came next if it hadn't been for Carlo.

'Look!' he yelled. 'There it is. I thought she was making it up, but it's real.'

There was no mistaking it. A large, dark blue

bus covered with golden stars was trundling down the busy street towards them. It had the Number 13 above its windscreen, and, being so starry, it matched the ticket Mrs Christmas had given them. Not only that, the stars on the bus all matched the star she had worn in her hair (except that none of them was tilted sideways).

Carlo shook his mother's arm. 'It's a Number 13 bus, Mum. There's a bus stop right here and — look — it's slowing down. Hey! It's looking for us.'

'Well I never,' said Jessica, hesitating at first. She made up her mind. 'All right! Why not? A fine day is one thing. The right bus stopping at the right bus stop at the right time is another. And we've got plenty of time for a joy ride. *You* give it a wave, Carlo. I'm all weighed down with soup bones.'

'I'm waving already,' said Carlo, and so he was. A minute later the wonderful dark blue and gold bus slid up and stopped beside them so they could scramble on board.

chapter two

THE BUS RIDE TO THE END OF THE WORLD

The driver was the most beautiful bus driver Carlo had ever seen. Her long green hair fell down her back like a waterfall, with yellowish strands shining among the green ones. She was wearing a dark blue dress (covered with golden stars) that came down as far as her feet, where Carlo could see she was wearing blue sandals. Her toenails were painted blue, and a golden star shone on each nail. Chains of leaves were plaited into her hair. She turned towards them, flourishing a ticket punch that looked as if it might be set with diamonds. When Carlo offered her the bus ticket she looked at it very carefully, and then studied Carlo and Jessica closely.

'So Mrs Christmas has moved on,' she said. 'We'll miss her, but never mind! We've all got to move on, and now we've got you instead. I'll just write you down in my book. It won't take a minute.' On a little shelf at her elbow sat an enormous book that looked as if it might be covered in moss. The bus driver opened it, and turned pages to somewhere in the middle. 'Names, please,' she said, and then she wrote down *Carlo* and *Jessica* with a great pen that seemed to Carlo to be writing with gold ink. But then the bus driver did something unexpected: she dropped down onto her knees in front of them.

'You don't need to bow to us,' said Carlo, but the bus driver wasn't bowing. She was looking hard at their feet, and pulled something rather like a magnifying glass from under her seat. She began studying their feet closely. At last she slid the glass back under her seat and stood up again. She was smiling.

'Better safe than sorry!' the bus driver said. 'I can't let just anybody onto the bus of course, or we'd have the bus filled with Dowlers in no time. They're good at disguising most of themselves, but it's hard to get away with forked feet, let alone claws, isn't it?'

Dowlers? Carlo wondered just what she meant — but he didn't like to ask, so he followed Jessica into the bus. The seats were covered with blue velvet, rather worn but very comfortable and clean, and scattered with silken cushions.

'What sort of a bus company *is* this?' Jessica was puzzled. 'I don't think I've ever ridden on a bus with *cushions* before.' They sat down carefully on the empty seat just behind the driver, and Jessica began to study the bus ticket very closely. There was fine print on the back, but, as Jessica looked at the words, trying to work out just what they were saying, they changed into tiny drawings — of beetles — and one word actually crawled off to the edge of the ticket and buzzed away. Jessica sighed and tucked the ticket into her shoulder bag and looked out of the window.

'I've never been down this road before,' she exclaimed. 'We must be getting out of town a bit . . . you'd expect the buildings to be smaller, but they're actually growing taller and taller.'

Outside, colour seemed to be draining from this unexpected part of the city as the buildings became not just taller, but greyer and more closed-in. The view from the bus was rather like the view from the flat, only there was a lot more of it. Windows were dark squares in walls of concrete block. Doors were shut tightly, and all looked as if they wouldn't open easily. Anyone trying to do business in this part of town would need lots of keys or maybe secret passwords. But, while Jessica looked out of the window, frowning at the grey buildings, Carlo began studying passengers in the bus, which turned out to be quite difficult. As soon as you looked at them, the other passengers seemed to melt into nothing. It was as if none of them wanted to be seen.

They came towards another bus stop and now Carlo could see — see quite plainly — a number of people shuffling and crowding forward. They certainly didn't melt away. But the bus sped up and drove right past them. Carlo glimpsed wonderfully dressed ladies and gentlemen, all new and smart, even though there did seem to be something strange about their stamping shoes. As the bus drove swiftly past them, they all began stamping, shaking their fists and baring their teeth. 'You missed some people,' Carlo called to the bus driver.

'I'm not taking that lot on,' she said. 'Dowlers, every one. And I ought to know — I used to belong to the Dowlers myself, back a bit before I changed for the better, so I'd recognize those shoes anywhere. They can disguise themselves all they like, but they can't totally disguise their feet. In under the leather and laces there are claws and cloven hooves. A bus driver gets to know.'

'There are a lot of other people on this bus. Are they all OK?' asked Carlo, looking around in a puzzled way. There certainly were other people in the seats behind him — but Carlo's eyes seemed to go round them in some way, or, just as he began to get them worked out, they disappeared. He could make out pieces of them — an eye here, a smile there — but never all of anyone. After a while he gave up looking, and turned back in his seat to study the bus driver in her starry dress, and to stare at the green striped hair falling down her back as far as her waist. All the same, parts of his head somehow began dancing with those bits and passenger-pieces he thought he'd seen in the seats behind him. A hand covered in blue fur? Could it be? Ears shaped like water lilies? Had he really looked into eyes like holes — but *watchful* holes? Or seen a smile showing a mouthful of silver teeth? What about that hat covered with flowers, leaves, praying mantises and grasshoppers? Or that head of wild curls threaded with beads and bells? Carlo was certain he had seen all these bits and pieces, but exactly whom they belonged to, or whether they were even really there, he couldn't tell. As soon as he looked away from them, they began to drift about like the leftovers of a wild dream.

Across the aisle of the bus someone was reading an enormous newspaper — a newspaper so big it totally hid the reader. Only fingers showed around the edges — thin, brown fingers covered with bright rings and ending with painted fingernails, each nail a different colour. Carlo was good at reading, but this newspaper didn't seem to be in any language he understood. Sometimes he thought he saw a word he almost knew. But, if he looked again, the word he was trying to see shifted down a line, or scuttled away over the edge of the page. It was impossible to catch on to any single word, so it was impossible to understand anything the paper was trying to say.

They drove on and on.

Carlo knew passengers shouldn't talk to a working bus driver but, as they drove, questions began fizzing inside him — questions that just *had* to get into the outside world and find answers for themselves. After all, asking questions was the only way to find out about things, and he was longing to find out.

At last he leaned forward. 'Who are the Dowlers?' he asked.

The driver didn't seem to mind him talking to her. 'Oh well, they're a big supermarket family,' she said. 'They're in the food-processing business and they own most of the alternative supermarkets . . . supermarkets in volcanoes or rat burrows — *that* sort of supermarket. But volcanoes and rat burrows aren't enough for the Dowlers. Oh no! They want to take over the whole lot — every single supermarket, even the Supermarket at the End of the World. And then, of course, we'd have to put up with rat-burrow groceries.' The beautiful bus driver made a sound rather like the growl of an irritated tiger.

'Dowlers or not, I'm enjoying this ride,' Jessica said. She was smiling a smile rather like the smiles she used to smile before Carlo got sick, a light-hearted and mischievous smile that curled around her face and tucked its ends into her dimples. 'Everything seems to have been so serious and troubling for so long. But today's different. First Mrs Christmas, and now a blue bus with golden stars.

It's fun being here. I'm glad *I'm* not a Dowler, even if they do own all the rat-burrow supermarkets.'

'The *alternative* supermarkets,' said the bus driver. 'And those Dowlers are nudging in . . . taking over . . . making everything the same. The food they stock — the breakfast cereal, the bread rolls, the cheese and the cherries — everything is made exclusively out of Dowler plastic and flavoured with Dowler dock leaves. They'll take over the world if we're not careful, and everything will be dowlerized.'

There was a little silence while Carlo and Jessica tried to work this out.

'Carlo and I just love this bus,' Jessica said at last. 'But isn't the road rather unexpected? Spooky, too. I don't think we've ever been this way before. All these buildings must have been deserted for years, and the air's beginning to look as if it's had a bit of golden syrup mixed into it.'

There was certainly a faint golden glow in the outside air — a sort of staining that softened the blind, shut-in faces the buildings were turning to the street. The gold deepened a little. The bus slowed down, drew into the side of the road, and stopped. There, in front of them, was a large street sign saying *THE END OF THE WORLD* in neat city-council printing. They must have arrived.

A feeling of movement ran through the bus as if those hard-to-see people were jostling their way out, mostly through the back door, though the newspaper reader certainly went out the front door, still reading his newspaper, though finding his way safely down the bus steps without so much as looking.

And yet, when Carlo and Jessica stood on the footpath at last, there was no one in sight. They were standing, side by side, in a soft, faintly golden haze, not so thick that they couldn't see perfectly clearly, but thick enough to make all edges around them a little smudgy rather than clear and sharp. There was a short length of road ahead of them, and then a line of very white trestles and orange road cones. A man in dark blue overalls stood there, looking at the bus in a thoughtful way. Beyond the trestles the road ended . . . well, beyond the trestles *everything* ended. There was a wide, smoky space, looking enormously deep. Jessica and Carlo, walking slowly towards the trestles, found that, somewhere across that misty space, they could make out yet another row of trestles, marking the beginning of yet another road and the vague shapes of far-flung buildings — the golden ghost of another city. 'Good heavens,' Jessica said. 'It really *is* like the end of the world.'

'That's because that's what it *is*,' said the man in overalls. 'Don't get too close to the edge, will you. It's a bit crumbly these days. But when people stop believing in things, then crumbling always sets in, doesn't it? Those things we forget to believe in begin falling to pieces . . .'

'And what's *that* on the other side?' Jessica asked, narrowing her eyes as she stared across the space.

'Oh well — it all begins again,' the man said. 'It's round, you know, the world is, but there's always this gap right here that you've got to watch out for. An end — yes — right! It *is* an end, but it's mixed up with being a beginning too. Some error in the planning stage, or a bit of industrial trouble a long way back . . . I don't know . . . I just do the warning-away, and light the lamps at night. Of course, that over there — that's another city entirely. I don't know anything about over *there*, only over *here*. And it's pretty quiet here. Most of us just do our jobs as well as we can, and then make straight for that comfy tea room inside the supermarket. Bliss!'

'We came here by bus,' Carlo explained.

'Everyone does,' the man said. 'The super-market calls to the ones who have bus tickets.' He pointed to a door. 'Funny place for a supermarket I often think, but it's fairly safe. The Dowlers haven't managed any sort of takeover. Not yet anyway! Well, not many of them actually get as far as this. Just half a dozen, say, every now and again.' And he held up his hands with his forefingers crossed, making a sign to warn all Dowlers away.

The door in the narrow wall didn't look anything like the door of a supermarket from the outside. It looked more like the back door of a building full of lost offices, or waiting rooms for shy doctors. But as Carlo and Jessica came closer, it flung itself joyously open, as if they were the very ones it had always been hoping for, and there, beyond the door, was a supermarket all right — no doubt about that.

chapter three

THE SUPERMARKET AT THE
END OF THE WORLD

Carlo and Jessica found themselves standing in a great echoing hall divided into aisles which were lined with long rows of shelves — shelves crowded with tins and packets, jars and bottles, along with boxes of all shapes and sizes. It looked like a supermarket all right, but it was rather more mysterious than most supermarkets as it was filled with shadows and echoing distances. Some of its aisles seemed to go on forever. There were several check-out counters, though only one was occupied.

A supermarket assistant in a dark blue smock sat behind an enormous machine . . . an adding machine, perhaps, but an adding machine so large and decorated Carlo thought it might be able to do a lot more than merely add up figures — as if it might offer good advice, along with a cup of coffee or an ice cream; might tell a fortune, perhaps; or sing a lively song or two.

Carlo and Jessica walked past the check-out point and into the spaces beyond.

'What a strange place,' Jessica said. Yet, once you were actually in it (if you ignored the echoes and shadows), it wasn't so very strange. It was — well, it was just a big supermarket. They walked and walked, and stared about them in silence.

'I think it goes on forever,' Carlo said at last. 'We could go on and on and *on* past shelves and shelves filled with supermarket stuff. Tinned pears and soap powder and pot cleaners!'

The ceiling, high above them, was lost in that same soft, golden gloaming they had seen in the street outside, and, as they moved past the shelves and looked down the aisles, Carlo and Jessica could see wide doors opening into shadowy spaces stretching out and up — just as far and just as high as the supermarket hall they were walking through — rooms and galleries, whole libraries and even apartments. Half-hidden stairs led down to sudden vaults where old plays and dramas might be re-enacted. Unexpected ladders climbed up to possible attics where Carlo felt suddenly sure music was being played and stories told. Sometimes, down one of those corridors, slightly smudged with golden mist, Carlo glimpsed a veranda or balcony where, it seemed to him, people were being welcomed or, perhaps, farewelled.

What he did *not* see was any edge or end. Once you were in it, the Supermarket at the End of the World really seemed to stretch out forever in all directions.

Carlo and Jessica were too shy to wander anywhere except in a straight line. After all, it would be easy to get lost in such a stretched-out supermarket. They simply followed those shelves loaded with bars, bags, bones and bottles, as well as hampers and hold-alls, including punnets, pots, pails, panniers, flasks, firkins and flagons, along with a great many canisters, cups, caskets, cruets, crates, crockery, creels, cartons and cardboard containers.

'The funny thing is,' Jessica said at last, 'we seem to be the only people here. So much stuff and so few customers.'

'There are a lot of other customers — well, I

think there are,' Carlo replied, 'but it's like it was on the bus — you only see bits of them.'

Indeed other people could be glimpsed, but always turning into the next aisle, vanishing around some convenient corner, or crossing from one room to another while pushing or pulling trolleys loaded with packets and plastic bags. And, once again, Carlo got the feeling that none of these people were quite ordinary. The bits of them he *thought* he saw seemed most unusual . . . paws instead of hands, eyebrows with little daisies growing among their hairs, knobbly noses and pricked, pointed ears.

'The brand names aren't what I'm used to,' murmured Jessica, picking a tin from the shelf and frowning at it. 'Do you know, I think that all the time we've been walking, we've just been passing different kinds of soup. Look at this one.' The label was headed with the words OPTIONAL SOUP in large blue letters and then, under that, was a long list in smaller print: Tomato, Cockaleekie, Mixed Vegetable, Turtle, Onion, Octopus, Gunpowder . . . and so on. 'Tick the desired flavour,' said a message along the bottom of the label. 'Heat and serve.'

'I'll take this,' Jessica said, shaking the tin. 'I

have to buy something for our lunch, and it seems cheap enough.' She stood there, staring at the tin as if it might argue with her. At that moment Carlo saw somebody who didn't duck out of sight, or vanish, or go all smoky when you looked at him. A man was walking along one of the aisles, and Carlo could clearly see the back of his dark head and his brown jacket. Beside him was a girl rather taller than Carlo, wearing ordinary blue jeans and a T-shirt. She had two fair plaits, looped and tied with blue ribbons. As Carlo stared, they hesitated at a tall display of bright packets, chose one, and then went on around a corner out of sight. But they had certainly been seen. There was no doubt about it — those people were *real*.

The sight of real people seemed to jolt Jessica out of her dream. She looked at her watch and cried, 'Oh goodness gracious me — we'd better get home. You're not supposed to do too much on your first day out, and we've walked such a long way already.'

'But we haven't got to the end of the super-market yet,' protested Carlo.

'Well, perhaps it hasn't got an end,' said Jessica, and then shook her head as if she suddenly had moths fluttering in her ears. 'What on earth am

I saying? Of course it must have an end . . . but right now we haven't got time . . . we just haven't got time . . .'

Nevertheless they wandered on just a little longer, passing trays of beads and badges, and wooden boxes lined with velvet from which spilled glittering necklaces and rings.

'Are they real diamonds?' Carlo asked.

Jessica answered him. 'They can't be.' But then she smiled and said, 'Well, perhaps they *can* be. A Supermarket at the End of the World probably has a bit of everything. I mean — look over there!'

She was pointing at a small set of shelves set apart from the others, surrounded by a tall wire fence. *Beware! Beware! And handle with care!* said a notice on the fence. There was a small skull and crossbones painted in the bottom right-hand corner of the notice. Carlo peered through the wire, a little anxious but very curious as well.

Burglar-Bite! he read. Rascal-Ruin! Pirate-Pongout! Horn-Hazard! Foe-Flattener!

There was another notice at the end of the shelf. *Keep away from parrots, monkeys and children*, it said in big red printing. Then in smaller printing it added: *If allergic to horror, avoid these remedies, or you may sneeze for a year. Free handkerchiefs supplied for the first two weeks. After that you must make do with your own.*

'Move on quickly,' said Jessica. 'You've sneezed enough lately.' So Carlo moved on quickly. He couldn't help being curious though.

At last, small in the distance, as if they were looking at it through the wrong end of misty binoculars, they saw the check-out counter once more, and the shop assistant sitting behind it, waiting for customers. He wore a dark blue smock, his shaggy green hair seemed to sprout out in all directions, and he was blowing bubbles from an old fashioned bubble-pipe while he waited. The bubbles streamed away from him like little glass worlds dancing around one another, signalling with rainbows then losing themselves in that golden haze under the roof. The man smiled at Carlo and Jessica, but, as they came up to his counter, a sudden crackling sound filled the air, and a very deep voice spoke out of a radio which Carlo now saw on one of the shelves behind the check-out counter.

'Attention, attention! A company of Dowlers has been observed, approaching in a nor-nor-easterly direction, driving in a convoy of Citroëns, Ferraris, Boscolas and Timpanisckas. They have half a dozen lawyers and two accountants in their leading car. May I have your instructions, please?'

The man at the check-out counter leaned forward and spoke into a hidden microphone. 'This is Sherwood Arden speaking. Follow plan A15 — obstruction with an unexpected circus parade, followed by a sudden heavy fog and change of road signs from Points D to H. You can distract those Dowlers with a few dreams and illusions if necessary — I'll leave that to your judgment. OK?'

'OK. Over and out,' said the radio, and it fell silent.

'Dear me,' Sherwood Arden said to Jessica and Carlo, who were waiting at his check-out counter by now. 'These Dowlers are getting very persistent. Very close too! Every now and then they do manage to get through, but only in ones and twos so far. I don't know what we'd do if a whole tribe of them made it. I'd probably have to use my gun — and I do hate violence.' He nodded at a very beautiful blue and silver gun hanging on the wall behind him. Carlo couldn't believe it would make much difference to a Dowler (whatever a Dowler might happen to be) if Sherwood Arden did fire it, for, in spite of its beauty, it seemed to be a pop-gun. Carlo could see the cork in the end.

Jessica put the tin of soup down beside the check-out counter till. 'Only one tin?' Sherwood Arden said, arching his eyebrows. 'You don't fancy our stock?'

'There were a lot of things we would have liked,' Carlo explained quickly in case Sherwood's feelings were hurt, 'but we have to make our money last to the end of the week and we've already spent too much. We had to pay for someone else's eggs.' He looked sternly at Jessica.

'Money is a terrible problem,' Sherwood Arden replied sympathetically, 'but we can't do without it, can we? And of course we supermarket people can't afford to give too many things away. Mind you, we do have a special today. Would you have room for a free tin of paint and a free paintbrush? We're overstocked with this particular line so we're giving free tins to every new customer.' Saying this, he passed his bubble-pipe to Carlo. 'Blow a few bubbles while I operate this machine.'

Jessica paid for the soup and the cash register accepted her dollar with a melancholy cough. 'Only a dollar!' it muttered in a gritty voice, then coughed again. A blue light flashed, a bell spoke with a deep single note, a yellow light flickered like sunshine on a butterfly's wing, and there was a little burst of music played on violins and penny whistles.

Carlo's newly blown bubbles danced upwards on the breath of the music. There were eight little ones and a big one, all slightly pink, barely blue, faintly golden.

'Goodness,' Jessica was saying, 'I hope your machine isn't too depressed by my dollar. It seems to have doubts.'

'All currency is welcome,' Sherwood Arden said. He had eyes like beads of green glass. 'We get all kinds here, and it sometimes takes the machine a little time to work out what it's been given. But it's a dear, faithful creature, even if it does get hiccups now and then.'

'Thank you so much!' said the gritty voice from deep inside the machine. It sounded rather sarcastic.

The man patted it again. 'Now, now,' he said soothingly, and added to Jessica and Carlo, 'It gets very touchy from time to time.' He leaned towards them. 'Due for an overhaul,' he added with a whisper and a wink. 'Now there's your soup. And there's your free tin of paint and your paintbrush. Don't get them mixed up. The soup takes a long time to dry, and the paint tastes rather bitter. And if you *do* happen to drink it, it sticks your teeth together.' He passed them a clinking bag, dark blue and covered with golden stars. 'And we value your custom. We hope to see you again in the near future.'

In the street outside, with its soft crumbling edges and golden air, the bus stood, waiting patiently. The man and the girl in blue jeans were just getting on board. Their backs were still towards Carlo and Jessica, but the brown jacket and the plaits with blue ribbons were unmistakable.

The bus driver was standing on the footpath beside the open bus door. 'It really *is* the end of the world,' Jessica said. 'It's amazing.'

'Well, after all, even the world has to end somewhere,' the bus driver said, clipping their ticket. 'Nothing goes on forever.'

A moment later they were sitting in the bus once more, going back towards the city they knew, and leaving the End of the World far behind them, bathed in its golden haze. Carlo looked around the corner of his seat, hoping to catch a glimpse of the man in the brown jacket and the girl with blue ribbons. He could see them sitting at the back of the bus, but the man's head was bent over, apparently looking at something on his knee, and only the top of the girl's head showed above the seat in front of her. All the same you could certainly see just where she was sitting because a ring of glassy bubbles bobbed in a circle above her. Carlo looked up over his own head and saw, for the first time, a tiny solar system of eight little bubbles dancing around a bigger one. There was no possible doubt: they were the very bubbles he had blown in the Supermarket at the End of the World, and they were following him home.

chapter four

A WINDOW WITH A VIEW

They got off the bus at the corner of their street and, all the way back to their brown flat, Carlo's bubbles followed them, bobbing and bowing in the breezes of the city . . . breezes made by passing cars and hurrying people. Sometimes it seemed those bubbles might burst or soar away over the roofs, never to be seen again, but then, somehow or other, they came back once more, following Carlo like good rainbow dogs, all the way back to the brown apartment.

After the wide and shining spaces of the Supermarket at the End of the World, their rooms seemed particularly small and dull. 'Oh well, we've had a wonderful morning,' Jessica said. 'We've been magical people for a little while.' She put her string bag on the table, took out the parcel on the top and looked at it long and hard. The blue and gold bag shone like a king's crown or pirate treasure sitting on their worn, scratched table top. The faint clinking, as the tin of Optional Soup nudged the paint tin, seemed full of promise. Then the tin of paint rolled out as if it were anxious to escape from the bag. The paintbrush edged out after it. Carlo picked up the paint tin and turned it around curiously.

'What *colour* is this paint?' he asked. 'Usually it tells you the *colour* of paint on the paint tin label, but this label doesn't say anything.'

'Let's have a look!' said Jessica. 'Grab a spoon and we'll lever the lid off. I'll bet it's blue with golden stars!'

As it turned out, the paint was a silver colour shot with streaks of blue and green. Carlo looked up at the ceiling where those bubbles of his still spun, glassy and mysterious.

'It's a sort of bubble colour,' he said. 'I wonder what it looks like when it's painted on. Shall we try a bit on the wall?'

'It could only make the wall prettier,' Jessica agreed. Her mischievous smile was back on her face. 'I've often thought we could do with a window right here.' She patted a bit of bare, blank wall. 'I wonder why I've never painted one before?' And, snatching up the paintbrush, she painted a streak of the paint onto the wall. Even when it was out in the everyday world, it was still hard to say exactly what colour that paint was . . . silver, yes! But other half-hidden colours too.

'Even if there was a window there it would only look through into the bathroom,' said Carlo.

'But suppose it didn't,' Jessica said, busily painting a big square on the brown wall. 'Suppose, by some Supermarket-at-the-End-of-the-World-magic, we could look through this window into — into some *other* place.' As she spoke she was turning that first square into a painted-on window frame, and, as he watched, Carlo found to his amazement that the brown wood within the painted square seemed to be thinning, fading and becoming transparent. Shapes were struggling to be seen. Strange streets and houses suddenly swam before their astonished eyes. Woody forms grew rounded, advanced, retreated, and then came forward once more. Figures moved. Slowly, like a photograph developing right there in front of them, the painted window came up with its own view, a view not of the bathroom but of an unknown city.

It certainly wasn't their own city, or a city either of them recognized, climbing in a staircase of white houses and shops up the sides of a rounded hill. In between the houses trees branched out, and other leafy trees lined the edges of every street. Birds and butterflies glided among the twigs. People were obviously living up among the leaves, with the branches full of platforms, ladders and tree houses. A face looked out at them, and Carlo saw pricked, furry ears and cat's whiskers, though the eyes of the face were as round and dark as his own. Other faces could be seen, looking back at him . . . peering up and then quickly down, as a procession of clowns and jugglers came winding along the footpath, in and out of the shadows.

One of the jugglers looked like Sherwood Arden, the man at the check-out counter of the Super-market at the End of the World, and he seemed to be staring straight up at their window, smiling at them, just as if he knew they were watching. He juggled oranges that shone like suns, and changed in the blink of an eye into yellow birds and red butterflies . . . turned into goldfish and then, almost before Carlo could be sure of what he was seeing, his bubbles bobbed in beyond that strange, painted frame, following the man as he followed the rest of the procession, juggling as he ran. Jessica and Carlo stared. Whiskery people came down out of their trees and some ran after the bubbles, others talked with people in the white houses across white walls, while still others worked on, planting flowers in among the roots of their tree homes.

Beyond the houses and the leaves you could see more green hills and a long arm of sea, stretching and rippling with blue muscles in between them, seeming to show off those muscle-waves by beckoning over and over again to Jessica and Carlo. A ship sailed across the blueness, swept along by a wind that billowed its squat white sails. The shadows of clouds flecked the hills, catching up with one another, then dissolving into nothing as Carlo's bubbles, which had now left the procession, drifted off among the trees. Carlo held out a hand, thinking he would feel warm sunshine in that mysterious place he was looking into, but his fingertips brushed against the old wooden wall. He could certainly see this strange city, but he couldn't reach into it.

'Nothing but the wall,' he said in a wondering voice. 'Did you *know* that paint would do that?'

'How could I?' Jessica replied. 'Carlo, all the time you were sick I kept on thinking *Why has this happened to us?* and I couldn't come up with any good answer. Now, when it seems we are having a very lucky, enchanted day, there's no answer to any *whys* about that either.'

'Why aren't you more surprised though?' Carlo said. 'I'm just totally, utterly bowled over.'

'I'm bowled over too,' Jessica told him. 'Mind you, I'm often bowled over by things much more ordinary than this. I'm amazed by all the stuff in any supermarket; I'm amazed by songs and singing; I'm just astounded by the different patterns of good and bad luck, and sometimes I'm never quite sure which is which — sometimes things that seem like bad luck turn into good. And now I'm going to tick *Tomato* on the Optional Soup and see what happens. And you must have a sleep after lunch, but, until then, you can look out of the window and enjoy the view.'

'Shall I paint another window?' asked Carlo.

Jessica paused, thinking, then shook her head. 'I feel you mustn't — well, you mustn't *hurry* enchantment,' she said, taking the tin of paint and putting it up on the end of the mantelpiece. 'You mustn't try to *force* it. You've just got to let it show itself to you when the moment's right. I think it wants to take us by surprise. I'll put that bus ticket *here* to go on with.' And she slid it into their dictionary — a most respectable, secure sort of book.

And later on the soup *was* tomato, and it was delicious. Through their new window a daylight moon stared across the green trees and white buildings, peering in at Jessica and Carlo as they enjoyed it, the moon probably just as surprised by their brown, cramped room as they had been by the round curve of the hills, and that unexpected, tilted town of white stone and green trees.

chapter five

A DOWLER VISIT

'Let's go to the Supermarket at the End of the World again today,' Carlo said eagerly, first thing next morning. It was still night-time on the other side of the painted window. Over there, everything was calm in the moonlight. Carlo wanted a bit more action.

Jessica paused in the middle of buttering toast. 'It would be fun,' she said at last. 'And I really want to go again, but, like I said yesterday, I think we need to be careful. Somehow I don't think we should *overdo* things. Anyhow, I've got to go to the post office and pay our phone bill. It's a bit overdue, but the Optional Soup was cheap and I've still got enough money to pay it. You'll be OK for about twenty minutes, won't you?'

'Sure!' said Carlo. 'I'm getting better every day.'

So, after breakfast, Jessica set off. But she had only been gone about ten minutes when there came a knocking at the door, though it sounded rather more like a slapping than a knocking. *Slap! Slap! Slap!* And at the edge of the slapping sound was another noise — a tiny, gritty noise that made Carlo think of a hundred impatient beetles scuttling across the door in shoes made of sandpaper.

Being the boy in charge, he went to answer that slapping scuttle.

A very tall woman was standing on their doormat. She was wearing a smart, lavender-coloured trouser suit, and a hat tilted forward over her eyebrows. Her hat was dark blue with silver stars pinned all over it, and to see her face properly, you had to crouch down a little and peer up under the brim. Her hands, one of which was still in a slapping position, had very long fingernails, almost like claws . . . all painted bright purple. It was her nails that had made the gritty sound.

'Hello!' she said, and then she seemed to lean forward a little, peering into the house over Carlo's head. 'Is your mother in?'

There was something about her voice, something about those fingernails, something about the way she loomed over him while peering *past* him as if he wasn't really there, that made Carlo feel uneasy.

'She's gone to the post office. She'll be back in a moment,' he told her. Under the brim of her tilted hat he could see the visitor's expression changing. She suddenly seemed as if she were in charge of the apartment, and of Carlo too.

'I'll just come in and wait for her,' the visitor said, stepping forward imperiously.

'I'm not allowed to let anyone in until my mother gets back,' said Carlo quickly, dodging sideways and getting in her way.

The visitor looked as if she just might reach over his shoulder, push the door wide and charge in, scratching her way past him, but then she sighed a little. 'Well, you might be able to help me. I think you've got something that belongs to me . . . something that was given to you by the one who *stole* it. And I want it back.'

'What sort of thing?' asked Carlo cautiously.

'Oh, nothing much,' she told him. 'Just a tatty old bus ticket. But it was a *hundred-ride* bus ticket with a few rides on it that hadn't been clipped. Give it back to me at once. I'd like it back *now*!' And she held out her hand, cupped so that her claws curved up under his chin.

Carlo didn't know quite what to say. He knew he wasn't going to fetch the ticket from the faithful dictionary that was guarding it so carefully. On the other hand he didn't want that purple visitor clawing him under the chin — or anywhere else. Claws like that might poison him. He looked down, pretending to be shy, while he quickly thought about what to do next. The woman leaned even further forward until he began to worry she might actually tumble on top of him.

'You can trust me,' she said softly. 'Look at my stars. You can see I'm one of the goodies. I've come all the way from the End of the World.'

But Carlo knew the silver stars on her hat were only pinned there. And then, as he desperately thought about what to do next, he noticed something else — something he hadn't noticed before, though he had been looking at her so carefully. The visitor's purple boots: they were elegant, high boots that reached up under the legs of her trousers, but the purple, pointed toes were split. To wear boots like that she must have cloven feet. And suddenly Carlo knew! He knew beyond any whisker of doubt. This visitor could be . . . *must be* . . . a Dowler!

Yes! There on his very doormat, peering into his very house, claws at the ready, was a Dowler trying to steal the hundred-ride bus ticket from him . . . the bus ticket that would take her to the Supermarket at the End of the World . . . the very supermarket that guarded itself so carefully from dangerous Dowlers. Carlo stepped back and slammed the door shut. As he did, the Dowler made a wild grab at him, but he was too quick for her. The door shut in her face, almost jamming her nose. As for her fingernails — four of them were caught in the door and snapped off, falling at his feet, where they lay twitching and clawing at the air like horrible beetles turned onto their backs. The key was in its keyhole inside the door. Carlo quickly locked himself in — and just in time, too, as the door handle twisted and then the door rattled wildly, so wildly it seemed it might split into pieces.

'Don't try and hide it from *me*!' the Dowler shouted through the keyhole. 'We're the ones who should have that bus ticket. We'll get it from you, even if we have to scrobble you into grit and gropple-grains.'

'Can I help you?' asked another voice on the other side of the door — a voice Carlo knew very well. It was probably the first voice he had ever heard. He sighed with relief. Jessica had come home from the corner post office, and just in time.

There must have been something about Jessica that bothered the Dowler.

'I was just trying to talk to your dear little boy,' Carlo heard the Dowler saying, sounding suddenly syrupy and sugar-sweet. 'But he is rather shy, bless his dear little heart. Never mind! I'll just go and — and come back another time.'

Then there was a sound of goat feet galloping away.

The door handle turned to the right, turned to the left, but Carlo was already unlocking the door. Jessica slid sideways into the room, glancing back over her shoulder. 'What was all *that* about?' she asked, looking apprehensive.

'It was a Dowler,' Carlo explained. 'A Dowler in our part of the world! She was after our bus ticket. But I was too quick for her. I slammed the door.'

'Good boy,' said Jessica. Then she danced sideways, pulling a face. 'Ugh! What are those — those twitching things down there?'

'Dowler fingernails,' Carlo explained. 'She was trying to grab me and I nearly caught her fingers in the door. They were crawling around a moment ago, but now they're just twitching.'

Jessica frowned, looking down at the fingernails. Then she laughed. 'Well,' she said. 'We *are* having a few adventures, aren't we? Let's enjoy them while we can.'

The fingernails twitched again, and grew still at last.

'Better sweep them up,' said Carlo, and he ran to the kitchen and scrimmaged for the dustpan and the little broom. He carefully swept up the broken Dowler fingernails, and dropped them into the fireplace.

'Let's have lunch,' suggested Jessica. 'These adventures have given me an appetite.'

'Me too!' agreed Carlo.

And he ate a bigger lunch than he had eaten in a very long time.

chapter six

AN UNEXPECTED MEETING

The next day started off just as every day had started off since he'd come out of hospital: Carlo had to stay in bed to begin with, then he was allowed to get up and get dressed, after which he had to take his brown medicine, his green medicine and his pink pill.

'I'm sick of taking medicine,' he told Jessica. 'I'm completely better.'

'Not quite completely,' said Jessica. 'But next week you can begin going to school again. Only three days to wait.'

Carlo found he was rather looking forward to school, which took him by surprise. School wasn't the sort of thing you were supposed to look forward to . . . well, not quite as much as *he* was looking forward to it.

'And today, after breakfast, you can go down to the corner shop for me,' Jessica told him. 'We need bread and oranges.'

'We should go to the Supermarket at the End of the World,' Carlo suggested. 'They might have oranges of gold.'

'Maybe tomorrow,' said Jessica. 'I keep telling you we don't want to overdo things. Anyhow I don't think gold has much vitamin C in it. Oranges are full of juice, and the juice is full of vitamin C, and a boy like you needs all the vitamin C he can fit inside him.'

Carlo thought that when it came to a place like the Supermarket at the End of the World there was no overdoing anything. They probably had whole bottles of vitamin C — whole kegs of it — along one of those mysterious, unexplored aisles. However, he ate his breakfast without further complaint, and then, unhooking the string bag from its special string-bag hook, he was allowed to go out into the world. Not heading for any strange supermarket this time, but instead for the little shop at the corner of Bread-and-Butter Street.

There were a few people there already, drifting

around and looking into the shop windows. Carlo slid into the doorway, and immediately felt that, in some strange way, he had arrived at the End of the World once more. Of course, in real life, he had just walked into the same old corner shop he knew so well. He recognized the same old counter . . . the same packets of biscuits on display . . . the same shelves of boring things like cornflour and baking powder. The things around him were all ordinary things . . . ordinary breakfast cereals, ordinary jam. The tins of soup were certainly not optional. All the same he had caught a glimpse of something he somehow recognized from yesterday's strange journey . . . something that had flashed before his eyes and then disappeared before he could quite tell what it was, just as the passengers on the bus had flickered on and off. There it was again, but this time it didn't disappear. Carlo had looked past it first time round. Now he saw it properly. A small, strong back and plaits of hair looped up with blue ribbons. The girl the ribbons belonged to was jigging from one foot to another, as if she were jumping in time to an invisible skipping rope — dancing to music only she could hear.

'Stand still, Pearlie!' someone told her — the woman next to her — a mother, probably, or perhaps an aunt, and the girl stood still, though Carlo could see she was secretly shuffling her feet.

He sidled up beside her. 'Hey!' he muttered, and she looked at him, looked away, then seemed to jump a little and looked back again.

'Interesting *buses* go past this shop sometimes,' Carlo said. 'Dark blue ones with stars. Do you have a ticket for a bus like that?'

Pearlie (for that was certainly the name the grown-up beside her had called her) stared at him as if he had said something wonderful but forbidden. 'Have *you* got one?' she asked, in a whispering voice.

'I haven't got it on me,' Carlo said, looking around just in case some Dowler was listening in on him. 'It's at home.'

'I've had mine for ages,' Pearlie replied. 'I've only got fifty rides left.'

'I haven't counted the rides left on mine,' Carlo said. 'If I use them up I suppose I'll have to buy another. Do they cost a lot?'

'You can't *buy* one,' said Pearlie. 'They have to be passed on.'

The woman beside Pearlie was walking away. Then she looked back over her shoulder, seeming a little impatient. 'Come on,' she called, as she walked out onto Bread-and-Butter Street. 'We haven't got all day.' Pearlie was about to be whisked away.

'Do you go to Ketchup Street School?' Carlo asked quickly, and she hesitated.

'I go to Kaviar,' she said. Kaviar was a private school for rich families, but at least it was close at hand.

'Pearlie!' the woman called from the shop doorway. 'Come on! I'm in a hurry. Hair appointment!'

'Her and her hair!' Pearlie said. 'All she thinks of is work and hair. Hair! Hair! Hair! She only has me staying with her to annoy Dad. Sometimes I wish she would go bald! Almost!' And then she was scurrying off after her mother.

Carlo saw them scrambling into a long, silver car parked at the side of the road. He felt glad Jessica tied *her* hair into a careless ponytail or simply let it dangle and tangle. Still, now he knew where to find Pearlie if he needed to. And next week he would be going to school again himself. Next week he would be part of real everyday life in the outside world once more.

chapter seven

BUYING BROWN SUGAR

'We're running out of brown sugar,' said Jessica, halfway through Saturday afternoon. She looked at Carlo. 'You don't have to tell me. Now's the time. Let's go.'

Carlo couldn't help giving a jump for joy, then ran to the bookshelf and took down the dictionary. As it opened, Carlo felt that, if books could smile, the dictionary would be smiling up at him. The hundred-ride bus ticket seemed to slide into his hand as if it had been waiting for his particular fingers.

'I hope we won't have to wait a long time for a bus,' he said, and Jessica laughed.

'Oh, I don't think we will,' she said. 'I think it's

a particularly quick bus service. I think the bus comes whenever you need it.'

And, sure enough, after they had collected the string bag and walked to the corner where Pudding Road ran into Bread-and-Butter Street, there was a dark blue bus patiently waiting.

Carlo thought it was the same bus they had ridden in last time, but, if so, it had a different bus driver: a young man in an ordinary bus-driver's uniform but with little antlers sprouting high on his forehead, just above his eyebrows — the sort of antlers a young deer might have grown. He did have green hair like the first bus driver, but his hair was very short. His head looked like a well-clipped, well-watered lawn with two leafless, wintertime trees on the edge.

'Show me your feet,' the bus driver asked them. 'Please,' he added.

Carlo held up his right foot. He and Jessica were both wearing sandals, so the bus driver could see their feet quite clearly.

'We're not Dowlers,' he said. 'We've both got ten toes on each foot — ten toes in fairly straight rows.'

'I didn't really think you were Dowlers,' said

the bus driver, 'but we've got to be sure. They can be very cunning these days. Very cunning! Very determined! They're getting closer all the time.'

Once again the bus swept through that strange, grey part of town, past doors and windows that looked as if they had not been opened for years, past walls crisscrossed with scaffolding, though there were no workmen balancing on the bars. Once again they stopped in front of that very ordinary door, and once again they found themselves walking between supermarket shelves that seemed to vanish into the golden, echoing distance.

'Brown sugar!' said Jessica. 'And we'll look around while we're here. There might be something else we fancy.'

Carlo was already looking around, checking the shelves of course, but at the same time, out of the corner of his eye, he was also looking for a possible Pearlie. He liked the idea of sharing the Supermarket at the End of the World with someone his own age.

'I'll get another can of Optional Soup,' Jessica said. 'We had three different flavours from that last can.'

'What about Possible Pudding?' asked Carlo, picking up a pink packet and holding it out to Jessica.

'Why not?' she said, dropping the pink packet into the string bag. 'Slop powder!' she exclaimed, about four shelves further on. 'I wonder if that gets dirty washing clean, or if it dirties clean washing? Well, I'm feeling adventurous, so I'll buy some and find out.'

They turned into another aisle and there, off in the distance, Carlo saw Pearlie. And, at the exact moment he saw her, she turned around and saw him.

Pearlie wasn't with her mother. She was with the man in the brown jacket — the one who had been with her before. They were looking at a shelf marked with a sign saying *Special*.

Within about seven steps Jessica and Carlo had caught up with them.

'This supermarket is so full of special things it's hard to believe they can describe any particular thing as *Special*,' said Jessica.

The man in the brown jacket turned around, smiling. 'I think this might be *especially* special,' he said. 'Look! Exploding Porridge! It might wake you up in the morning. Or perhaps it would protect you if you were attacked before midday. But I think you'd have to be particularly brave to have Exploding Porridge for breakfast, don't you?'

'We *are* particularly brave,' Jessica said, smiling as she dropped a small bag of Exploding Porridge into her string bag. 'We might try it during the weekend.'

The man in the brown jacket looked at her with admiration. 'Exploding Porridge! Wow!' he said. 'What courage! Let me know how you get on.'

'Where's your mother?' Carlo asked Pearlie in a whispery voice.

'Mum? She doesn't believe in this supermarket,' Pearlie explained. 'But I can come here whenever I'm staying with Dad. My Mum and Dad don't live together any more — they're divorced, so they have to take turns with me. I'm their great, wonderful treat. Weekends with Mum — well, mostly — because she works during the week. She's a supervisor.'

'It looks as if there's a tearoom through there.' Pearlie's father was peering cautiously around a stand which advertised Paragon Pizzas. He pointed at it. 'Look!' Then he read aloud: 'Tongue-twisting tantalizingly tasty treats, trickled with tomato, toffee, tamarillo, treacle and tapioca, all tarted up with tender tapeworms. Wow! I'd feel nervous going into a tearoom like that on my own — but if I had company . . .' He smiled at Jessica.

'All right! Let's protect one another,' said Jessica. Carlo could tell Jessica liked the thought of a bit of tearoom protection herself, particularly when the protector was wearing a brown jacket with dashing silver buttons.

Pearlie and Carlo followed their grown-ups through golden space into a room filled with tables and cushiony chairs. They seemed to be the only people there — well, almost the only people, for Carlo kept seeing bits of several someone-elses . . . an eye that blinked out when he looked over at it, a nose which was being wiped with a yellow handkerchief, and which then sniffed itself away, vanishing into nothing. Just beyond the vanishing nose he made out a mop of hair like streamers of willow, blowing out around a face it was impossible to see properly. But though it was hard to work out just who was sitting around them in the tearooms, it was easy to hear that the teacups, laid out on the tables, were all rattling just a little, as if they were just longing to be filled with tea.

'This table seems to be empty,' said Jessica,

though she did not sound entirely sure. 'Come on, kids! Sit down!'

So they all sat down. At first, sitting down in the billowing end-of-the-world tearoom chairs seemed like slowly falling into some sort of soft nothing, but then, before any of them had time to be truly alarmed, they found that softness cuddling in around them, while invisible hands arranged cushions and propped them up and in. They all sighed with happiness.

But then, just as they were beginning to feel at ease with the room around them, something rather alarming happened. A hairy ball bounced out of a door and came rolling towards them, and, within a moment, they all saw it wasn't really a ball but a *head*, its eyes wide open under dark, straggling eyebrows, and its mouth seeming to smile when the head was the right way up, but seeming to turn down crossly when it wasn't. Happy-grumpy-happy-grumpy, it tumbled towards their table.

'Who are *you*?' cried Pearlie's father, leaping to his feet as if he was getting ready to protect them all from something dangerous. '*What* are you?'

The head's mouth opened. 'I am your waiter,' it said in a deep, respectful voice. 'Your *head* waiter.

May I take your orders? Tender tapeworms are our special for the day.'

But not one of them wanted the tapeworm special. Jessica ordered a pot of tea along with scones and blackberry jam and whipped cream for everyone. Pearlie's father, whose name was Dominic, ordered a lot of little cakes decorated with sugar-flowers. Pearlie and Carlo asked for tall glasses of orange juice with rainbow ice cubes. It seemed you could easily get things like that in the Supermarket at the End of the World. Dominic and Jessica now began to talk over the heads of the children the way grown-ups often do, which meant Carlo and Pearlie could have a private, lower-down conversation of their own.

'We had a Dowler try to get into our house and steal our bus ticket,' Carlo told Pearlie.

'They've tried to get ours too,' Pearlie said. 'A Dowler came pretending to sell raffle tickets for a good cause. But he couldn't hide his feet; his shoes were shaped like hooves.'

'Our Dowler was a bossy woman with her hooves half-hidden in high-heeled boots,' Carlo told her. 'Purple ones! I don't think they can ever utterly hide their feet, not even in gumboots or they'd wear gumboots all the time.'

A waiter suddenly appeared beside their table. She was carrying one tray, very carefully, using both hands, but she had another tray with a teapot, a little milk jug and a sugar bowl balanced on her head. When she reached their table, she whistled. Dishes leaped from the two trays. Within a moment their table was neatly laid with the teapot, flowery cups on matching saucers, two very tall tumblers tinkling with rainbow ice cubes, and other delicious bits and pieces set out on blue plates with starry borders.

They had a wonderful afternoon tea, sitting in those soft, cloudy chairs, breathing in the golden air, while, all around them, possible people and animals blinked in and out of existence.

And, at last, everything on the table was finished, and there was nothing left to eat or drink.

'Time to go home,' said Dominic, sounding just a little sorry to think their afternoon tea was over. They stood up and walked back through the golden light of the supermarket, out through the little door and into the city beyond.

A blue bus was parked at the supermarket bus stop. But, as they walked towards it, something quite unexpected happened. A whole gang of people descended on them, shouting and hooking long, painted nails at them.

Dowlers!

These Dowlers weren't pretending to be ordinary people, and weren't dressed in ordinary outside clothes. They wore orange pyjamas, split down the back and Carlo could make out hairy skins and spikes along their spines — spikes that lifted and fell . . . lifted and fell.

'Give us those bus tickets!' the Dowlers yelled. (They were not only Dowlers; it seemed they were Howlers as well!) 'Give us those bus tickets or we will claw you to pieces!'

'What are we going to do?' yelled Carlo, but at that moment there was a great bang, just as if a cannon had been fired. And then another. And then another! Jessica dropped her string bag. It leaped on ahead of her like a small kangaroo, but she ran after it and snatched it up again. 'Behave yourself!' she told it firmly. There was yet another explosion.

Carlo couldn't work out just what was going on. Who was shooting whom? Then he saw the Dowlers were all sliding to a stop and rubbing their faces wildly. And no wonder . . . their faces suddenly seemed to be plastered with soft, dripping, grey mud.

'Quickly! Quickly!' shouted a voice. It was the

bus driver who had driven them to the End of the World earlier, now dancing at the door of the blue bus and flourishing his card clippers as if he were waving a sword. As Carlo and Jessica, along with their new friends, ran for the bus, both Jessica and Dominic began waving their hundred-ride bus tickets, ready for clipping.

Clip! Clip! They were into the bus, and the bus driver jumped in behind them.

One Dowler, less blinded and confused by the grey mud than his friends, sprang in after them, but the bus driver put his head down and, using his little antlers, skilfully tossed him up and out. The Dowler slammed against the top of the bus doorway, then, turning a mid-air somersault, tumbled out into the street, falling flat on his back.

A fall like that would have bothered most people, but the Dowler leaped up immediately. It was as if Dowlers could bounce, or perhaps that particular Dowler had a spring hidden somewhere between his shoulder blades. He sprang at them, hooking his long nails as he sprang. However, by then the driver had cleverly closed the bus door. The bus gave out a musical roar, then sprang away like a blue elephant escaping from wolves. The leading Dowler — the one who had stretched out his claws at them — missed the bus and fell over yet again, but flat on his face this time.

'Wow! That was close!' cried the bus driver. 'They're certainly moving in on us.'

'What happened back there?' asked Jessica, looking rather confused. 'Who shot that wonderful mud all over the Dowlers?'

'You did!' said the bus driver. 'That wasn't mud, it was porridge. The right kind of porridge can be a wonderful weapon. Read our history and you'll find a whole chapter on the Porridge Wars.'

Jessica and Carlo, Dominic and Pearlie all stared at him as if they couldn't believe what they were being told. Then Jessica began to search through the groceries in the string bag. 'It's gone!' she said at last in a bewildered voice. 'The Exploding Porridge I bought is all gone.'

'Exploding Porridge is very intelligent,' said the bus driver. 'And it's Dowler-sensitive. If it detects a Dowler, it aims itself and then it boom-splats! You did the right thing buying some.'

'Exploding Porridge!' said Dominic in a reverent voice. 'I'll get some myself next time.'

'Is it *all* gone?' asked Carlo.

Jessica held up a limp bag. 'Not quite,' she said.

'There's a little bit left in the bottom of the bag, but we'll need to get some more next time. And — oh blow! I forgot to get brown sugar, which was why we came to the supermarket in the first place. The Exploding Porridge distracted me.'

'Ah,' the bus driver said. 'This is the sort of bus that goes back again if you forget anything, and then it waits for you. It's very well-trained. Let's go and get your sugar! The Dowlers won't be there this time round. Not after that porridge attack. They'll have to scrape porridge off their faces, and it's very sticky when it sets. Like glue! Scraping-off can take ages. Mind you, I've probably got a bit of Dowler dust on my antlers, but I won't have to scrape. I'll just wipe it off when I get home tonight.'

Later, as they set off for home for the second time in ten minutes, brown sugar in the string bag beside them, strange and wonderful music came out of the air above. They drove back through the city feeling restful, and not only restful — thanks to the bus and its obliging bus driver, they all felt safe as well.

The time came for Jessica and Carlo to leave the bus.

'Thank you so much!' Jessica said to the driver. 'I wish I had antlers like yours.'

'It's been a pleasure,' said the bus driver. 'And I think you can get Antler-Gro at the supermarket if ever you're brave enough to go back again.'

'Oh, we're very brave,' Jessica said. 'But I don't know about the Antler-Gro. Exploding Porridge probably suits us better.' She turned to look at Dominic and Pearlie. 'I wonder what happens if you have Exploding Porridge for breakfast,' she said. 'We might try it and report back to you.'

'Better be a bit careful,' said Carlo. '*We* might explode ourselves.' He looked at Pearlie. 'See you next time!'

'Right!' said Pearlie.

'See you next time!' Jessica said to Dominic.

'Right!' he answered, smiling. And then, holding their end-of-the-world groceries, they went their separate ways.

chapter eight

HUNTING DOWN PEARLIE!

Carlo had a quiet Sunday at home. He didn't ask Jessica if they might go to the Supermarket at the End of the World because he knew by now she would say they mustn't overdo things. And by now there were so many other things to think about.

He was beginning school again on Monday, and that school was still a new school to him. He had only been there for two weeks before he had been taken ill, and, though it seemed to be a friendly school, he hadn't had time to get to know anyone really well. Of course, now he had met Pearlie and, though they had only spent a little time together, he felt he had made at least one real friend in that new part of town.

It is true that particular friend was a girl, and he had only been with her for just a bit over an hour or so, but that was long enough to know a few things about her. Pearlie was not only an adventurous girl, she was a girl with a hundred-ride bus ticket. She had to count as an ally, even if she didn't go to the same school.

Sure enough, on the Monday Carlo went back to his new school, and Jessica went with him, just to remind the teachers who he was. As they walked briskly down Sandwich Road, Carlo found himself staring hard at a particular building. He'd noticed it before, but now he was noticing it with new interest.

It looked rather like a castle, its windows peering cautiously at the world across a tall stone wall with gates curling like iron serpents in the middle. *Kaviar College* said an elegant sign bolted to the front of those gates with silver bolts, and Carlo remembered that Kaviar College was Pearlie's school.

He slowed up a little, studying it carefully, but Jessica hurried him on.

'We mustn't be late,' she said, as if she were

going to school too. 'Ketchup Street should be the next on the left.' And so it was.

Ketchup Street School was set in large green grounds with several big trees springing up out of it. It had a small brightly coloured playground in one corner with an orange slide and four swings — red, blue, yellow and purple — along with a big, round, curling pink and white tube with a plastic cat at one end and a plastic dog at the other. Kids could crawl in at the cat, wind around and around in the tube, and then, at last, come out at the dog.

Jessica and Carlo walked past the playground to the school office. Jessica spoke to a woman sitting behind a desk, then led Carlo to his classroom — Room Number Five — and to his teacher, a sprightly woman called Mrs Morrison.

'I'll collect you after school,' said Jessica. 'Be good, Carlo. Stay well, and have a happy time.'

Mrs Morrison was a kind teacher, and the other kids in the class were quite friendly. The day passed quickly and after school, sure enough, Jessica was there to meet him, just as she had promised.

Of course on the next day Carlo had to walk to school on his own — and walk home on his own when school was over. Life had been very busy over the last couple of days, what with getting ready for school and so on, and he hadn't had much time to think about dark blue buses, Exploding Porridge or ferocious Dowlers.

But on the afternoon of his second day at school, wandering home alone, he suddenly found himself staring at the curling Kaviar College gates and at the Kaviar College pupils coming through them, probably all making for home just as he was. They wore dark green blazers and dark green berets, and looked unnaturally tidy for kids on their way home after a day at school.

'Kaviar hogs croak like frogs!' some of the pupils from Ketchup Street School shouted across the street.

Most of the green berets turned away from the Ketchup Street gang, but three or four of the Kaviar College pupils began a war dance and sang back: *'Ketchup fools bray like mules!'*

A girl beside Carlo turned to him and said, 'You're a new kid, aren't you? We hate all those Kaviar College cranks. They all think they're better than us.'

Carlo was trying to think of something to say when, there among the Kaviar College pupils, he noticed Pearlie, looking a bit like a walking springtime tree in her green blazer and green beret. She was staring over at him, and, when she saw he had seen her, she flipped her hand at him in a secret wave. He thought she had something hidden in that hand.

Because he was a new boy with no close friends among the Ketchup School pupils around him, Carlo had no trouble in slowing down and drifting back from the crowd. He could see that, over on the other side of the street, Pearlie was doing the same thing. There was a shop on the Kaviar College corner, and, giving her hand that secret flip once more, Pearlie disappeared inside. The Kaviar College pupils moved on, some of them exchanging shouts and insulting rhymes with the Ketchup Street gang.

The traffic lights at the corner turned green. Carlo had to wait while energetic cars sped past. At last there was a safe crossing space and Carlo ran across the road. Casually he wandered towards the shop. He looked left . . . looked right. No Kaviar College or Ketchup Street pupils close to him. Carlo went into the shop, just as Pearlie had done a few minutes earlier.

There she was, looking thoughtfully at the

chocolate bars displayed on the counter, but as Carlo came up to her, she turned away from the chocolate and flicked her hand at him for the third time. Now Carlo could see she really *was* holding something . . . something she wanted to show him. It was a slightly crumpled, dark blue bus ticket.

'I've been looking out for you,' she said, 'all day yesterday and today, and here you are at last. Shall we catch the bus and go to the supermarket on our own? No Dad! No Mum!'

Carlo immediately knew this was exactly what he had been wanting to do all day. However, he also felt rather anxious at the thought of actually doing it. 'Might be a bit dangerous,' he said. 'Just you and me against — well, say . . . a gang of Dowlers.'

'We'll just have to be too clever for them,' replied Pearlie. 'Also, probably whichever bus driver is on will help us to smash them.'

Carlo thought for a moment — or perhaps he was just *pretending* to think, trying to trick himself into seeming sensible.

'Anyone we meet, we'll study their feet,' Pearlie went on. She laughed at herself. 'Hey! I'm a poet, and I didn't know it.'

'OK! Let's go,' said Carlo. 'But I mustn't be long, or Mum'll worry. We'll wait at the bus stop until a bus comes along and then . . .'

'We won't have to wait,' said Pearlie. 'Look out there!'

Carlo looked out through the shop doorway and saw a big, blue bus drawing up just outside the shop. It was as if the bus ticket had somehow secretly whistled it in.

The driver of this particular bus also had green hair — but Carlo was used to that by now. All the same, this green hair gave him a great surprise, for as he climbed the steps into the bus, every hair on the bus driver's head reared up and watched him. Every hair on this driver's head turned out to be a tiny green snake, hissing, then twisting and twining into curls, before rearing up once more and hissing again. Pearlie gasped and stepped backwards onto Carlo's foot — the same foot Mrs Christmas had stepped on. Limping a little, Carlo pushed in front of Pearlie.

'Excuse me,' he said to the bus driver, speaking very politely indeed. 'Are you a Gorgon?' Jessica had read him stories about people who had snakes instead of hair, and he had suddenly remembered what they were called.

'My grandmother was a Gorgon,' said the bus driver. 'Grandma G! So gorgoning runs in my family, just like bus driving. My grandfather was a bus driver and so was my father before me. My mother too. I may have inherited Gorgon hair, but I've also inherited bus-driving skills. I drive exceptionally well. You'll be safe with me.'

She clipped Pearlie's card twice, and Carlo and Pearlie slid once more into the bus. It flickered with other possible passengers.

'Weird!' said Pearlie, sinking down into her blue velvet bus seat, and speaking in the sort of contented voice people use when they come home after a long day.

'Does your dad let you use the card often?' Carlo asked curiously, as they drove through the city. Pearlie was staring out at the grey buildings . . . at those closed windows and doors.

'No way!' she said. 'But I stole it two days ago so I could use it today. Dad always says we mustn't overdo the Supermarket at the End of the World, but I want to know everything about it. I want to know it by heart.' She turned and smiled at him. 'I've been looking out for you. I thought you probably went to the Ketchup School. I knew you didn't go to mine. I saw you yesterday, but your mum was with you and I wanted you on your own.'

'My mum's great,' said Carlo.

'Mine's all right,' said Pearlie, but she sounded doubtful. 'I mean, I think she almost likes me but she's always flat-out busy, even in the weekends, and I get in her way. She's a sort of ex-mum. My dad's terrific though, and he believes in the Super-market at the End of the World. He really loves it.'

Outside, those tall, closed-up buildings seemed to drift past, and then drift past again. But at last they arrived. They were at the End of the World once more. They scrambled off the bus, waving goodbye to the Gorgon bus driver.

'I wonder how she *combs* her hair?' said Pearlie as they made for the small door they knew so well by now.

'I think she would have a special comb,' said Carlo. 'I'll bet you can buy snake-combs in this supermarket.'

Once again they found themselves looking for astonishing signs, as they breathed in deeply, enjoying that golden air. *Have a snack in the bath!* suggested a poster on their left. *Wash yourself with soap-and-raisin biscuits! Wash first, then eat!*

They passed the aisle that led to the tearooms, but neither of them had brought any money. They could explore, but they couldn't buy anything. And then . . .

'Look!' said Pearlie, pointing to a notice neither of them remembered seeing before.

We are testing our seaside sandwiches, ice creams and ding-dongs said the notice. *Try them! Taste them! Test them! Tantalize your tongue with our tempting treats. No payment required. Totally free!'*

'I think *my* tongue wants tantalizing,' said Pearlie.

'What does *tantalizing* mean?' asked Carlo a little cautiously. 'I mean it *sounds* all right, but that might be a notice put up to trick Dowlers.'

'Let's find out,' suggested Pearlie, and she set off past the notice along an aisle that glowed just slightly and, every now and then, actually sparkled. Carlo followed her. They were surrounded by shelves filled with tools — hammers, spanners, saws, boxes of nails and a variety of powerful yard-brooms.

At the end of the aisle they came to a counter covered with open boxes and great glass jars that seemed to be filled with blue and green smoke.

Swimming in that smoke were a lot of different shapes, but it was hard to make out if they were the shapes of sweets or cakes or little biscuits. The supermarket assistant standing behind the counter smiled at them.

'Can you two be tempted by terrific-tasting treats?' she asked, offering something crimson to Carlo and something plum-purple to Pearlie. 'Domestic dainties, delicious as honey-dew-dip dumplings!'

'But these aren't dumplings,' said Carlo, peering at his crimson shape. 'And they aren't sandwiches or ice creams. What are they?'

'We call them ding-dongs!' said the assistant. She wore a dark blue smock embroidered with golden stars. 'Try them!'

Carlo hesitated. 'I — I haven't got any money,' he told the assistant.

'Neither have I,' said Pearlie.

'These are free samples,' the assistant replied. 'We think you will enjoy them so much you'll bring money with you next time and buy several boxfuls.'

So Carlo took his crimson ding-dong and Pearlie took her plum-purple one. A moment later Carlo felt he had been taken over by such sweetness that it seemed he might be dissolving in the flavour. Sweet — yes! Sweet, but not too sugary. There seemed to be a touch of unexpected lemon mixed into the sweetness, a little sharpness that somehow made the sweetness seem sweeter than ever.

'Gosh, ding-dongs are —' Pearlie began, pausing, smiling, and licking her lips, so Carlo knew she had tasted that sweet-sharp taste as well.

Carlo was about to ask if there were any other free samples when something unexpected happened. The tiled floor twitched. Some tiles burst into pieces which flew high into the air, then crashed into the aisle behind them. Bang! It seemed as if some kind of trap door was forcing itself open under their very feet.

'Ding-dongs!' cried a hoarse and hideous voice. 'Ding-dongs! I demand ding-dongs! Deliver those ding-dongs!'

'Dowlers!' screamed the assistant. 'Dowlers darkening our doors! I mean forcing our floors!'

And sure enough, a Dowler began twisting up out of the hole it had made by breaking through the tiles.

Carlo found the sweetness of the ding-dong

has somehow filled him with courage. He began to sing, dancing a war dance:

'*Ding-dong-diddle-dong! Ding-dong-dee!*
There isn't a Dowler as clever as me.'

He grinned at Pearlie. She grinned back and then she sang too:

'*Ding-dong-diddle-dong! Ding-dong-duss!*
There aren't any Dowlers as clever as us.'

They were both ready for adventure.

chapter nine

BEATING AND DEFEATING THE DOWLERS

'But,' Carlo shouted to Pearlie, 'it isn't enough to sing about being clever! We've actually got to *be* clever!' Yet again, a clitter-clattering fountain of tile-scraps flew into the air.

Carlo swung around, staring desperately at the shelves behind him. Then he grabbed up a big yard-broom from the broom stand, and swung it down on the Dowler's head.

'Here's a ding-dong for you!' he shouted.

The Dowler let out a scream of rage and tried to guard the top of his head with his hands. But, as he did this, Pearlie leaped into the battle. She grabbed up two hearth brushes from the box beside the broom stand and beat on the Dowler's head, rather like a drummer drumming hard on a drum. The Dowler's skull gave out notes like a gong. The Dowler screamed again, but this time there was terror as well as rage in his scream.

'Don't beat me on the boko!' he cried. 'My boko might explode!' and he dived back under the broken tiles.

'Quickly!' said Carlo, looking wildly about the shop. But Pearlie was ahead of him, trying to push a heavy stand hung with stainless-steel saucepans over the hole in the floor.

The wail of the beaten-down Dowler rose up from under the floor, along with other Dowler howls and yowls. The voices echoed and rang from one saucepan to another.

'Run!' shouted Pearlie. 'They might leave the supermarket alone if we aren't in it.'

So Carlo and Pearlie took off at the double, speeding from aisle to aisle, armed with brooms and watching out for any other Dowler breakthroughs.

'Attention!' said the supermarket radio. 'Dowler subterranean penetration in the tool area! Dowlers beaten off by courageous customers! All supermarket assistants, arm yourselves with brooms and watch the floor!'

'Pearlie!' shouted a man's voice.

'Carlo!' shouted another voice — a mother's voice.

In the next moment Dominic had grabbed up Pearlie, and Jessica had clutched Carlo's arm. She held it so tightly his fingertips got pins and needles.

'How dare you come here without me!' shouted Jessica.

'How could you be so *silly*!' Dominic yelled at Pearlie.

'Mum, we were *fine*!' Carlo shouted back.

'Dad, we were clever. We beat the Dowler down!' yelled Pearlie. 'We both *broomed* him.'

'Soldiers should carry brooms as well as guns,' said Carlo, rather more quietly. 'Brooms are really useful.'

'The army should have a special broom-battalion,' added Pearlie.

'Look,' Jessica also sounded rather quieter this time around, 'this supermarket is full of goodies, but it's full of dangers too . . .'

'*Hidden* dangers!' put in Dominic.

'Full of *dangers*!' repeated Jessica. 'You're not to come here without your parents. And it's like I've told you. This is a great place, but we mustn't overdo things. If we use up our bus tickets, we'll never be able to get in here again.'

'Well, *you* got in,' said Pearlie, looking up at Dominic, 'and you didn't have a bus ticket, because I had ours.'

'But I shared *ours* with him,' explained Jessica. 'I rang him when Carlo was so late home from school. And you were late too, Pearlie. We were really worried about you both.'

'But they were so brave — brave and useful as well,' said a voice, and there was their first bus driver, leading a supermarket trolley, piled with remarkable things, past them. She wasn't pushing or pulling it — it was just following after her like a good dog. 'These kids beat back an actual Dowler. Of course they shouldn't have come here without useful parents, but I've never seen such skill with a yard-broom.'

And having said this, she strolled on by towards the check-out counter.

'It's such a relief to have found you safely,' said Jessica. 'Look, you kids don't deserve any treats . . . but let's go to the tearoom. Dowler-danger has dried out my throat. I absolutely have to have some sort of refreshment.'

'Good idea!' said Dominic very heartily. So off they went. And once again they had a wonderful time.

chapter ten

SLUG-PIRATES

When you know there is an end to the world (after which it begins all over again), when you know there is a supermarket (filled with everything ordinary along with everything marvellous) waiting at the End of the World, and when you have a bus ticket that allows you to catch the bus that takes you there, then it is hard not to think of it every moment of every day. Having the right kind of bus ticket was wonderful. And another good thing happened too: Carlo's friend from his last school — his friend Harding — began to call in on him.

'Carlo! Pay attention!' said Mrs Morrison. 'You say you are feeling a lot better now, so you must start your school work all over again.'

Carlo knew this was true, but, as he sat at his desk, supermarket pictures kept flowing out of his memory, and though those pictures were almost like dreams, somehow they seemed to be truer than anything in the everyday world. At times the blackboard, the desks and the maps of New Zealand on the classroom wall felt as if they were part of a world he was inventing, while the Supermarket at the End of the World, floating around like a dream in his head, felt completely real. He must get back there. He must.

'No! I must stick to true life,' he told himself sternly, but, immediately, true life seemed to be all Optional Soup and Exploding Porridge — something you could only buy in the Supermarket at the End of the World.

These days, Harding would sometimes catch up with Carlo walking home from school. And sometimes Carlo would see Pearlie on the other side of the street, looking as green as spring in her school uniform. They would nod knowingly at one another across the street. *'The time will come again . . .'* sang Pearlie, so loudly he could hear her words in spite of the traffic that roared between them. *'Soon! Soon!'* he sang back.

'What are you on about?' asked Harding.

'Just inventing a song,' Carlo said quickly, and he sang again:

'*When will I fly up as far as the moon?*
Soon! Soon! Soon! Soon!'

He sang loudly so his song would be heard on the other side of the street.

'Being sick has made you a bit crazy,' Harding said.

Very frequently these days Carlo and Jessica began their dinners with Optional Soup. The label on the tin was covered with ticks. Carlo was surprised to find himself enjoying Octopus Broth, but both he and Jessica were rather scared at the thought of ticking the word Gunpowder — Exploding Porridge had made them cautious. And the Possible Pudding, which Jessica had bought on their second visit, was utterly delicious, but confusing too. You couldn't be sure just what sort of pudding it would turn out to be. Though it often looked like mere pink oatmeal to start off with, it sometimes tasted like ice-cream cake, and sometimes (though there was no juice you could see) like fruit salad made with pineapple and passion fruit.

The weekend came.

'We need more Optional Soup,' Carlo said slyly.

Jessica laughed. 'Well, we do,' she agreed. 'Would you like to ring Pearlie and Dominic and see if they are interested in catching a bus — a blue bus with golden stars on it, if we can find one?'

'Those buses find us,' Carlo reminded her.

As he said this, the phone rang. Jessica answered it.

'Jessica here,' she said. Then she listened and laughed. 'That's funny!' Carlo heard her saying. 'We were just going to ring you. Good idea! What time? All right! There's no time like immediately-now.'

She put the receiver down and looked at Carlo. 'That was them. We're off and away,' she said. 'Well, we will be if we can be ready in about three minutes.'

'I'm ready now,' Carlo said, but he had to wait while Jessica quickly put on some lipstick. He thought she took more care than usual and, though she had already done her hair that morning, she did it all over again, pulling it this way and that until, at last, she was happy with herself. They set off, side by side, only to find the bus already waiting for them at the corner of the street. Pearlie was peering down through a window at the back, grinning and waving at them.

This time the bus driver was a man with hair like lettuce leaves. Dark green leaves hung around his ears and tender, pale green leaves sprouted from the top of his head. 'Wonderful to see you again,' he said as he clipped their bus tickets. 'It seems quite a long time since you last used this bus. We thought you might have been frightened away by the Dowlers.'

'No way!' Jessica exclaimed. 'The Dowlers should be frightened of us. It's just that we don't want to use up the bus ticket too quickly.'

'Very wise,' said the bus driver. 'Some people overdo things, and overdoing is often disastrous. Those people who overdo their bus tickets — well — they sometimes turn into Dowlers themselves, and spend the rest of their lives trying to steal someone else's ticket so they can get onto the bus again.'

'I guessed that,' said Jessica. 'Well, I almost guessed it.'

Then Jessica and Carlo pranced down the bus, past other odd, flickering passengers, to the seats at the back.

'Hooray! Here we are again,' said Dominic. 'Terrific to see you both.'

'Here's to us all, and here's to the End of the

World!' cried Jessica, flinging her arms wide before settling into a bus seat. She nearly toppled over, but Dominic held up his arm, reaching across Pearlie, so Jessica could catch hold of it and balance herself.

'Here!' said Dominic. 'You and Carlo sit over there, Pearlie. Then Jessica can sit by me. You can have your sort of gossip and we can have ours.'

There was a scuffle at the back of the bus as they shifted around.

'Isn't it great?' Pearlie said to Carlo, when they had settled down side by side. She looked quickly back over her shoulder. 'I've always wanted life to be exciting, and going to that supermarket — well, that's very exciting because you never know what's going to happen next.'

'I'm getting a bit used to it,' Carlo told her. 'Being surprised, that is.'

'But every time is different,' said Pearlie. 'I mean, we've been through this part of town two or three times by now, but . . .' She looked side-ways at Dominic and Jessica, then she leaned towards Carlo. 'I think we're being followed!' she whispered. 'Look out of the back window. No!' she hissed as Carlo began to twist in his seat. 'Make out you're looking backwards by accident. And don't say anything much, or them there : . . .' (she jerked her thumb secretly backwards at Dominic and Jessica who were talking cheerfully), '. . . they'll get all scared like a good Mum-and-Dad, and they might make us get off the bus and walk back home.'

Carlo pretended to wriggle and stretch a bit. Then, slowly, he looked to the right. He looked to the left. And, at last, he twisted lazily around and glanced out of the back window.

Another bus was bowling after them — not an End-of-the-World blue bus, and not a city bus either. It was a black bus, its Headlights shaped like skulls with crossed bones below them. Headlights like that would have looked terrifying glaring out at night. Even in daylight they had a very threatening appearance. Carlo could easily see they were being followed by a pirate bus.

'It's been after us for a while now,' Pearlie said. 'I think whoever's on that bus is tracking us, and probably planning to rob our supermarket. And I reckon a crew of piratical Dowlers could easily be travelling on a bus like that, don't you?'

Carlo was sure she was right. 'I think Dowlers could easily turn into part-time pirates,' he agreed. 'What will we do? Tell the driver?'

'I think we'd better,' said Pearlie, and she stood up bravely. Carlo stood up as well.

'No walking around while the bus is moving,' cried Dominic and Jessica, a duet of stern parents.

'We *have* to,' said Pearlie, but then she shouted down the bus to the driver. 'Hey! There are bus pirates after us!'

By now they were bowling between those tall grey walls, along a street wide enough for a lot of traffic but which seemed, right then, to be entirely empty apart from their bus and the pirate bus behind them.

As Pearlie spoke, that pirate bus sped up and spun out onto the wrong side of the road, just as if it were planning to pass them. But instead of passing, it kept on driving alongside. And as Carlo and Pearlie stared at it in dread and astonishment, a window rolled down and a steel ladder shot out from somewhere inside.

There was the sound of breaking glass. The ladder had smashed its way in through one of the windows of their own bus. And, immediately, strange black-bus-pirate passengers began scrambling out over the ladder, trying to cross from one bus to another.

Carlo blinked. There at the other end of the ladder, peering out along the ladder from inside the black bus, he could make out a couple of Dowlers. However, the creatures sliding across the ladder towards them certainly weren't ordinary Dowlers, and if they *were* pirates, they were very peculiar pirates indeed. They looked rather like huge black slugs. On they came, and on again, oozing . . . oozing . . . crawling slowly but steadily. The Dowlers in the black bus shouted and waved, urging them on. 'Go, slugs, go!' they were yelling, and the slugs *were* going! Slime dripped down from them onto the road below. 'Yo! Ho! Ho!' the slugs were howling. 'It's slime time!'

'Hey! Shoot away down a side street,' Jessica called to the driver.

'No side streets in this part of town,' the driver called back. 'Walls, walls, walls. A few doors and windows, but all locked! No such thing as side-ways!'

The slug-pirates — slimy and horrifying — slid steadily along the ladder-link. It was as if the Dowlers were squeezing dangerous black toothpaste from one bus to the other. But the unpleasant smell coming in the broken window certainly wasn't a toothpaste smell. It was more like the smell that comes out of an old rubbish tin that hasn't been emptied for weeks.

'Give in now, or we'll grind you to gropple-grains,' the slug-pirates began crying in strange slip-slop voices as they crawled towards the blue bus, two or three on the top of the ladder, others hanging down beneath it.

'Gropple-grains! Gropple-grains!' shouted the Dowlers through the black-bus window. Their voices seemed to leap-frog from one slug to another, and then run along the ladder ahead of them.

'Well, nobody's grinding me to gropple-grains!' shouted Pearlie. 'What'll we do?' she muttered sideways to Carlo.

'Push the ladder back out!' Carlo cried, standing up in rather a wobbling way, because the blue bus was rocking a bit as it raced along.

'Great idea!' yelled Jessica. 'Clever boy! He must take after me. Come on, everyone!'

Dominic and Jessica, Pearlie and Carlo closed in on the end of the ladder and began shoving wildly at its steely end. However, the ladder was jammed in very tightly. Though they all heaved as heartily as they could, the ladder wouldn't move back a single bit.

'Gropple-grains! Gropple-grains!' hissed the slug-pirates, oozing ominously on . . . on . . . ever on. Though they moved slowly, by now they were very close.

'Slop them! Slime them!' shouted the Dowlers back in the black bus.

'Can't you help us?' Jessica called to their driver.

'I have to keep the bus on the road!' he yelled back. 'I mustn't drive up onto the footpath. Or slam into the side of a building. That would be awkward. Illegal too.'

The two buses, the blue and the black, raced on side by side along a street that seemed to have no ending.

'Yo! Ho! Ho! Gropple-grains! Gropple-grains!' wheezed the slithery slug-pirates in their horrible voices. The leading slug-pirate was almost at the window of the blue bus by now.

'There's only one thing for it,' the driver cried. 'Emergency escape! Back to your seats and put on your seat belts.'

A bus with seat belts? Carlo could hardly believe it. But, when he looked over at his seat, there, sure enough, were seat belts looped so neatly you would hardly notice they were there.

'Quickly!' shouted the bus driver. 'Emergency rules!'

Dominic and Pearlie, Jessica and Carlo scrambled for their seats, and clicked themselves in safely.

'Yo! Ho! Ho! Gropple-grains! Gropple-grains!' The first slug-pirate was already squeezing in through the window. The broken glass didn't seem to worry it at all. It must have had a very tough skin under all that slime. The black bus tooted mockingly, and the Dowlers cheered.

Carlo couldn't see just what their driver did, but suddenly their bus tilted in an astonishing way. It reared up onto its back wheels, and the driver seemed to rise into the air above them, while the tall grey buildings fell away below. From somewhere in front of them — out on either side of their bus — great feathered wings were unfolding and flapping. The whole bus shivered, and then they were actually flying. The ladder was wrenched away from the black pirate bus, and suddenly the slug-pirates were wagging wildly in the city air.

'Yi! Hi! Hi!' they cried despairingly. The ladder swished backwards and forwards, and two of the pirates tumbled away, screaming and probably swearing in slug-pirate language.

Up went the blue bus, then up again, up and out of the city, which was now spread out below like a coloured board game.

'Mercy!' screamed the pirate who was halfway through the broken window.

'Down with all Dowlers!' shouted the bus driver.

And, at last, the end of the ladder that had been pushed through their window shifted. At last it tilted sideways. At last it broke free. Over and over went the ladder, tumbling and bumbling away from them, while those pirates who had been still clinging to it (including the one who had been halfway through the window), whirled off in all directions.

The bus wobbled a little, but somehow balanced itself. Within a moment they were spinning over the city, safe and serene.

'What on earth . . . how did you do that?' cried Dominic.

'Don't worry, I have a pilot's licence,' the driver called back. 'And there's a landing strip on top of the supermarket. You're safe with me.'

It was so strange. Only a moment ago everything had been so desperate and dangerous — they had seemed bound for disaster. And now, suddenly, everything had changed. Here they were, flying high in their blue bus set all over with the golden stars. Flying! Flying serenely! The bus glided like a gull, then swooped like a hawk.

'Oh! Look at that view!' the driver called as they swung down.

And indeed it was a wonderful view. The city stretched out lazily below them, the river curving like a question mark, through the middle of all the shops and factories, houses and apartments which now stood out like jumbled words, telling the story of the city. Beyond the city the sea took over, its long waves moving majestically, carrying secret messages in towards the land.

'It's like a printed page,' said Jessica. 'It's as if the sea and the city are both telling stories.'

Those long waves did indeed seem like lines on a page . . . lines in a mysterious, salty language which no one but fish and mermaids would ever be able to read.

'I think it *is* a story all right,' Dominic agreed. 'An old, old one!'

'A story that goes on and on — no ending yet,' said Jessica.

'If we keep on flying, and if we keep looking down, we might be able to work it out,' said Carlo.

'See that wave breaking over there? I think it's saying *Once upon a time*!'

But the flying bus was leaning sideways in the air, and the strange, salty sea-and-city-story edged out of view.

'Keep your seat belts on!' the driver shouted as the bus glided gently over the roofs below.

'This is almost as comfortable as sitting on those cushiony chairs in the tearoom,' said Carlo, as they flew off towards the End of the World.

There was a slight bump. The bus jolted a little, ran forward a little, and stopped.

'Here we are, safe and sound,' the driver called. 'While you do your shopping I'll fix that broken window. Oh, and watch out as you go downstairs. There just might be a Dowler or two, trying to find a way in from above. They seem to be attacking from all directions these days.'

chapter eleven

THE ALMOST-PARTY-PLAN

The bus had landed on the top of a tall building. The strip upon which it had landed was as smooth as a bowling green. A narrow brick path ran alongside the landing strip, leading to a big trap door, painted blue. That trap door looked as if it hadn't been opened for years, but as Carlo and Jessica, Dominic and Pearlie walked towards it, a powerful (but slightly out-of-tune) note of music chimed around them, and the trap door lid rose slowly and majestically, then wobbled backwards and forwards, almost as if it were beckoning them on.

'A staircase!' cried Carlo. 'Down!'

'Of course,' Pearlie said. 'We're on the tip-top of everything. There's no way to go but down.'

They reached the trap door, and began to scramble downstairs.

In some way the staircase on which they now found themselves was unexpected, for it was made of a rich, brown, highly polished wood, rather like stairs in some magnificent old house. A dark blue carpet embroidered with golden stars ran down ahead of them, so clean and new it looked as if no one had ever trodden on it before.

'No way to go but down,' Pearlie said again, so down they went. The walls on either side of them were hung with pictures of wild meadows, ships tossing at sea, castles on mountains, and lions stretched out, half hidden by wild grasses. The strange thing was that if you stopped and really looked at those pictures, you could see the wind ruffling the lions' manes and swaying the grasses, and you could see the ships were actually moving, tossing up on one wave then sinking down again, up and down, up and down. But of course Pearlie and Carlo were too interested in getting to the supermarket to take much notice of wind-blown lions or wild oceans, all held in their own spaces by picture frames.

The stairs came to a stop, but Carlo and Pearlie were not in the supermarket — not yet. They seemed to be in a great cave, its walls painted with mammoths and bears. Old! Very old! Carlo looked around rather nervously, worried some hairy caveman might suddenly leap out and challenge them.

Dominic was fascinated. 'Imagine this in the middle of the city,' he said. 'We could spend hours exploring this cave.'

He sounded so very interested that Pearlie was afraid the cave was taking over and Dominic was forgetting the supermarket.

'Look! More stairs!' she cried, pointing, and there were indeed more stairs, stone stairs this time, going down into a darkness broken up every now and then by big, branching brackets of candles that seemed to be growing, like living boughs, out of the wall.

'Let's press on,' said Jessica. 'We'll explore this cave some other time.'

So they went on down the stone stairs, and came to yet another floor. This time it seemed they were in a short street lined with tiny shops, some of them as small as broom cupboards. Was the street empty, or busy with shoppers? It was hard to tell. Just for a moment you could see someone, or part of someone, but then that person you *thought* you were seeing vanished into some shop, or wavered, winked and went out like a blown candle.

'We could do a bit of shopping here,' suggested Jessica.

'No, let's press on down,' said Dominic. 'I expect the supermarket is down *those* stairs.' He was pointing at yet another staircase that fell away straight in front of them.

This staircase was the strangest of all, for it seemed to wind down through the branches of a tree — indeed sometimes the branches of the tree were the actual steps of the staircase. Music of different kinds came in on them as if there were musicians hidden among the leaves. Birds were singing, and sometimes you could see those birds — small birds, bright as feathery jewels, all singing wonderfully as they watched Dominic and Jessica, Carlo and Pearlie climb on down . . . down . . . down.

The stairs narrowed and turned into ladders zig-zagging down a tree trunk. And when they got to the bottom of the last ladder they saw the tree was growing out of a huge pot, a little chipped around its edges, and there was yet another ladder going down from the rim of the pot to the ground below.

'Where are we now?' asked Carlo, though he

knew that no one, not even his mother, could be sure. They seemed to have arrived in a short hall — a hall with a pointed ceiling, draped with graceful lace curtains of spider webs. There was a door at its far end, and of course they made for that door, which opened politely as they came towards it. Light burst through, welcoming them, inviting them in. Carlo went first and Jessica followed him, and there it was . . . they were inside the supermarket at last.

They had come in at the end of a long aisle. On either side of them were shelves loaded with goodies. And there were the shadows of those other shoppers who always seemed to be going around some corner or somehow melting, along with their well-behaved trolleys, into those long, crowded shelves.

'I wonder if those others can see us,' said Carlo. 'We might just flash on and off to them the way they flash on and off to us.'

'Let's buy something,' said Pearlie. 'Something delicious! Something really strange!'

'Well, of course,' said Jessica. 'That's why we come to a supermarket, isn't it?'

They began their shopping.

'What shall we get now we're here?' Jessica asked.

'Let's get some good things to eat, and take them round to *our* house,' suggested Dominic. 'Let's have a — well, not a party exactly, but . . .'

'An *Almost*-Party!' cried Pearlie.

Jessica nodded and smiled, agreeing with Pearlie.

Carlo hesitated. 'Why do we have to have an Almost-Party?' he asked. 'We escaped from the slug-pirates. We could celebrate, and have a total, entire, actual party.'

Jessica frowned thoughtfully. 'I still think we mustn't overdo things. I mean we mustn't act like tourists, just looking things over. And we mustn't have a party every time we escape from the Dowlers. We must save that party for some truly marvellous time — some time when we manage to be utterly astonishing or lucky. When we've beaten the Dowlers down forever, or something like that.'

'Don't let's argue, anyway,' said Dominic. 'Let's just see what we can buy today, and then have that Almost-Party at our place — just to go on with.'

'Look!' cried Pearlie, pointing. And, strangely enough, there above the next-door aisle, was a sign, shaped like an arrow and pointing firmly down the aisle. It read *ALMOSTS* in flowing capital letters. Underneath this single big word were smaller ones: *Almost-Adventures, Almost-Excitements, Almost-Parties*...

'Terrific! Exactly what we're needing!' declared Dominic. 'Grab a trolley.'

'Where are the trolleys?' asked Carlo, looking around, but at that moment something nudged his elbow and, when he turned to see what it might be, he found a trolley sidling up beside him. It must have known it was needed.

'Got one!' Carlo shouted, and he and Pearlie almost ran into the aisle beyond that pointing sign.

'No Exploding Porridge,' Jessica called after them. 'Porridge just doesn't fit in to an Almost-Party, especially if it's going to explode.'

'What does fit in?' asked Dominic.

'Let's find out,' Jessica answered, and she and Dominic eagerly followed Carlo and Pearlie into the ALMOSTS aisle. The shelves there were filled with strange objects. Under a sign advertising *Almost-Adventures* were Almost-Guns, Almost-Treasure-Maps, Almost-Shipwrecks, Almost-Gorillas and many more Almosts.

'Don't look at those,' Jessica ordered quickly. 'We might try Almost-Adventures next time around. Right now we only want Almost-Party things.'

Almost-Parties said a sign over the next block of shelves.

'Here we are,' cried Carlo. 'Look! Lots of tapes! Almost-Singing! Almost-Jokes!'

Pearlie was a little ahead of him, holding what looked like a jar of jellybeans. 'Tablets for Almost-Dancing,' she read, then held the jar over her head and rattled it rhythmically.

'We don't need those,' cried Jessica. 'We can almost dance without them — and we can *really* dance, whenever we need to.'

'So we can,' said Dominic. 'We should try dancing together sometime.' As he spoke he actually danced a step or two there in the ALMOSTS aisle of the Supermarket at the End of the World. Jessica stepped up to him. He put his arms around her and they twirled about together.

'That's *real* dancing,' Pearlie said. 'Stop it — we're shopping for an Almost-Party. Look, Almost-Strawberry-Juice, Almost-Cake, Almost-Candles!'

'Almost-Balloons,' Carlo frowned at the packet he was holding. 'How can a balloon be almost?'

'Only one way to find out,' said Dominic. 'Let's buy some.'

'Almost-Fizzlepop,' said Jessica. 'I wonder what Fizzlepop is? Something to drink, I think. Hey, let's get some Almost-Fizzlepop and find out for sure. It sounds Almost-Party-ish.'

'Almost-Popplefizz,' said Dominic, pointing to the next shelf along. 'And look, Almost-Chocolate.' He quickly grabbed a block of it and put it into the trolley.

'What do you think of this?' cried Carlo. He was looking at a big packet shaped like a birdcage. 'Almost-Parrots! Do parrots fit into a party?'

'Some parrots perhaps.' Jessica looked doubtful. 'Into some parties, that is.'

'And Almost-Parrots might fit into Almost-Parties!' Pearlie did a dance step of her own around the cage, reading the Almost-Parrots instructions as she danced. 'Spread Almost-Birdseed on the most Almost part of your kitchen floor. But there's nothing *almost* about our kitchen. Dad wipes the *almost* pieces away with a damp cloth.'

'There's plenty of almost in ours,' said Carlo. 'A lot of days we almost turn the dishwasher on . . . well, we would *really* turn it on if we remembered to do the dishes. But we forget. And then, when we do remember to turn it on — well, it doesn't quite go — it *almost* goes.'

'As for us, we don't always have cake in the house,' said Dominic, staring down at a packet of Almost-Cake. 'Only *almost* always.'

'Here's the Almost-Birdseed,' cried Carlo. 'Let's take two packets in case we get it wrong the first time. I'd hate to miss out on the Almost-Parrots.'

'I think we've got enough,' Dominic said. 'We'll have to be careful or our Almost-Party might turn into a real party, and that's not what we had in mind.' He turned to Jessica. 'We've got a big house with a big lawn,' he said. 'But if we do have a lot of fun — if we make a lot of noise or laugh a lot — our next-door neighbours complain. They're a dull lot.'

'Mainly the man on the left,' added Pearlie. 'And we have to do what he says: he's a policeman.'

'That's funny,' Jessica said. 'If *we* make a lot of noise, our landlady, who lives in the flat above us, knocks on her floor, which is *our* ceiling, with a broom. It's just as if we were Dowlers trying to break up through her floorboards.'

'It's just as if she was a Dowler trying to break down on us,' said Carlo.

'Neighbours!' they all said together, sighing and smiling just a little sadly.

'Would Almost-Neighbours be better or worse?' asked Carlo, but no one was sure.

'Anyhow, who are we going to invite?' Pearlie, who had been dancing along, came to an almost-standstill. 'If we ask our friends, won't that make it a real party, not an *almost* one?'

'But we can't ask enemies,' cried Carlo.

'Good point!' Jessica said. 'Dominic and I will think it over.'

They came up to the check-out counter, Carlo dragging the parrot cage after him. A tall woman was waiting for them. She had blue hair and there was something odd about the way she looked at them. Carlo couldn't work out quite what it was for a moment, and then he saw that she had three eyes . . . two quite ordinary blue eyes, one on the right and one on the left, but she had a third eye, a beautiful brown one with long lashes all around it, just over her nose. When she began to help them take their goods out of the trolley, she shut her blue eyes and counted the goods with her brown one.

'You must be planning an Almost-Party,' she said.

'We are,' Jessica agreed. She hesitated and then said, 'Would you like to come?'

The woman's blue eyes suddenly popped open, sparkling like rare jewels.

'I'd love to,' she said. 'When are you having it? And where?'

'Tonight at my place,' Dominic told her. 'I'll give you my address. And there might be a few more supermarket people you'd like to bring with you.'

'I'll ask around,' the check-out woman said. 'We working people aren't supposed to go to actual parties in case we get home all worn out and sleep in the next morning, but an *Almost*-Party — well, that's a different matter.'

'Mum, why did you ask her?' whispered Carlo as they wheeled the trolley out through the door of the supermarket.

'I just had the idea that she might be a good guest for an Almost-Party,' Jessica replied. 'She's a bit of an almost-person herself, isn't she? Look! There's the bus, just waiting for us.'

And there, indeed, it was, its stars glittering in the sun.

'Oh! You must be having an Almost-Party,' said the bus driver as they climbed onto the bus, loaded with parcels, and with Carlo and the parrot cage coming last of all.

'We are,' replied Carlo and Pearlie, speaking together.

'Would *you* like to come?' asked Pearlie.

'And bring a few other bus drivers?' asked Carlo.

'How very kind of you,' said the bus driver. 'We know just where you live, of course. You've got onto the bus more than once by now, and you're in our records. We can be there on the stroke of twelve.'

'Make it earlier,' said Dominic quickly. 'An actual party might begin at midnight, but an Almost-Party starts a lot earlier.'

'I should have thought of that,' said the bus driver. 'We'll call in at half-past-seven. How's that?'

'Perfect!' said Dominic. 'We'll really enjoy seeing you front-on. In the bus we mainly see your back.'

They sat down on the blue velvet seats. The bus started, sang, and whirled them away from the edge of the world through those grey streets, between those grey walls, and on and on until they stopped, at last, outside a house which Carlo knew must be Pearlie's home.

chapter twelve

FIZZLEPOP, POPPLEFIZZ AND PARROTS

Pearlie's house was big, old and white with a red roof. It was surrounded by trees, and other trees spread out leafy arms and marched up and down on either side of the street, so it was as if Pearlie and Dominic lived in the heart of an almost-forest — a *city* forest but, all the same, a forest full of mysteries. It reminded Carlo of the forest he could now see in the painted frame on the wall of his own brown apartment-home, but if he put out his hand to touch these trees he would feel true bark under his fingers. The moment he saw those trees he longed to be out climbing one of them. On one side of the forest was a hedge, and on the other side of the hedge a green roof.

'That's where *he* lives,' said Pearlie. 'Old Poppadom, our neighbour. The policeman who complains if he hears us having too much fun!'

'I'll bet he doesn't hit on your ceiling with a broom,' Carlo said. 'Mind you, that was what gave me the idea of grabbing a broom to hit the Dowlers.' As he said this, he was following Jessica, who was following Dominic along a path through a half-weeded garden and onto a wide veranda. Carlo was pulling the cage for the Almost-Parrots after him, and it made a funny clattering like a tin man laughing.

'You've neglected your poor plants,' Jessica told Dominic, looking down at those weeds.

Dominic sighed. 'It's a busy life,' he replied. 'I get halfway through a lot of things, and then something else pushes in on me, and I have to forget all the first things and get on with the next ones. And Pearlie's mostly at school. I need sympathetic support.' He gave Jessica a melting glance.

They climbed onto the veranda and waited while Dominic unlocked the front door. As they waited, Carlo looked back towards the gate — and froze. Something was moving out there on the other side of the hedge. The hedge was much too thick for him to be sure just what it was he had seen, but he knew at once that they were being spied on. He was suddenly glad the front door (which Dominic was now opening for them) was so very thick and strong.

They came into a little hall. The carpet was blue, but not dark blue, and without any stars; rather, it was exactly the colour of a midsummer sky.

'In here,' said Dominic, opening another door into a sitting room, with green carpet this time, and chairs as tawny as lions, with arms stretched out on either side of them, like great soft paws, and pale walls patched with pictures.

'Dad painted that one — and that one,' said Pearlie, pointing. She started to dance a little. '*Great that you're here! Great that you're here!*' she sang.

'Hey there!' Dominic said. 'Not too much noise. Remember we don't want our Almost-Party to turn into an actual party. We'll have an actual party when the policeman next door is off and away, but for now let's stick quite firmly with an Almost. And let's go into the kitchen and check out just what we've bought from that wonderful supermarket.'

So they went out into the hall again (Carlo still dragging the parrot cage), and through another door into a big kitchen, bright with cups and plates on a wooden dresser, and shining with a fridge and cooking stove that looked almost new.

They opened the Almost-Chocolate first, and found squares made up of a lot of other little squares — all rather like real chocolate squares but coloured purple and pink. Not only that, each little square had a picture of a bird on it. Dominic and Jessica began breaking the big squares into little ones and putting them into small glass bowls. As they did this, Carlo and Pearlie tore the wrapping off the parrot cage and read the instructions.

'Sprinkle Almost-Birdseed on the floor of either kitchen or cage. Then stand back!'

'There's too many of us treading around the kitchen,' Dominic said. 'We don't need parrots, or even Almost-Parrots, crowding in on us. Leave Jessica and me to work at the bench. You two can experiment in the corner over there.'

Carlo and Pearlie opened the packet of Almost-Birdseed and sprinkled it all over the cage floor. Then they stood back, and waited eagerly for some Almost-Parrots to appear. Nothing happened.

'Maybe the Almost-Birdseed is a bit *too* almost,' said Carlo at last.

'Or maybe it isn't almost enough,' suggested

Pearlie. 'Shall I try some more?' But at that very moment she was distracted by Dominic and Jessica reading out the instructions on the Almost-Fizzlepop box. 'Find a large bowl or a big stewing pot. Fill with cold water. Empty the Almost-Fizzlepop pills into the stewing pot and stand back.'

'Easy!' cried Pearlie and, opening a cupboard door, she pulled out a great pot which looked as if it hadn't been used for a long time — it had a spider web stretched across it.

'That's a soup pot not a stewing pot, but it'll have to do,' said Jessica, brushing the web away with her sleeve. Then Dominic and Jessica talked grown-up talk over Pearlie's head as she hoisted the pot up onto the bench and pushed it under a kitchen tap. Dominic helped her lift it down when it was full. After all, a big soup pot full of water is very heavy and easy to spill.

'Now . . .' said Jessica, opening the Almost-Fizzlepop box. It was filled with small pills that seemed to be coated with silver.

'Drop some of them in!' Dominic said. 'Then we'll see.'

So Jessica dropped about half of the silvery pills into the soup pot.

'You keep an eye on this,' Dominic told the children. 'We'll have a go at baking the Almost-Cake.'

So Carlo and Pearlie waited. They didn't have to wait for long.

Soft music arose from the soup pot. The water inside it began to shine with a silvery sheen. Then bubbles began to rise. The bubbles blew themselves up, reflecting the kitchen around them, before bursting softly. It sounded as if the kitchen was crowded with musicians, all softly plucking the strings of violins or magic banjos.

Meanwhile Dominic and Jessica had begun working on the Almost-Cake which foamed up in the middle of a big yellow plate, forming something that looked like a chocolate rosebud — almost, but not quite. It swelled, then swelled again, growing bigger and bigger, and then opened up like a great chocolate rose, offering its petals to anybody who might want one. Indeed it was hard to refuse . . .

'Wait,' said Jessica. 'We've invited people, so we mustn't eat everything before they come. Look! Here's another Almost-Cake. And another one.'

Carlo and Pearlie went back to start working on the Almost-Popplefizz. This time round, Pearlie pulled out a big crimson bowl from another cupboard. There were no spider webs on this one and it looked very festive. She filled the bowl with water, and Carlo quickly sprinkled in the Almost-Popplefizz pills. Immediately the kitchen was filled with a curious fizzling sound — rather like the sound of frying bacon. The Almost-Popplefizz pills had looked just the same as the Almost-Fizzlepops in their silvery way, but they behaved very differently. They bounced up and down on the top of the water, and began fizzing and singing in voices as thin as threads but as clear as little daggers of polished glass.

'Pop my fizzle and fizzle my pop!
We'll keep dancing till we drop!
We will dance like sparks of fire.
Higher, higher, higher, higher!
We never groan, or grouch or grizzle!
Fizzle my pop! And pop my fizzle!'

The water in the pot turned a soft blue, sparking with light and making a fizzling sound which was all its own.

And at that very fizzling moment, there came a sudden screech . . . and then another . . . and then another. Carlo and Pearlie, Jessica and Dominic spun around. They had forgotten the parrot cage, which was now swaying wildly from side to side, and no wonder! It was jam-packed with little round eyes, hooked beaks and claws, as well as bright feathers going in all directions.

'Parrots!' exclaimed Dominic. 'I've always wanted a parrot.'

'You've got your wish then,' said Jessica. 'Almost! Or perhaps ten times over! Hard to tell which.'

'They're too crowded in there!' cried Carlo.

'Don't let them out. They'll fly around and poo in the Almost-Fizzlepop,' called Jessica, but she was too late with her good advice, for Carlo had already opened the cage door, and suddenly the air was whirring with parrots — well, Almost-Parrots, for these parrots were even brighter than actual parrots. It was as if someone with particularly colourful pencils and paints had coloured them in. Every feather seemed to be a slightly different colour from the feather next to it.

'Our Almost-Party will be an Almost-Parrot-Party,' said Pearlie, as a parrot perched on her head.

'Polly wants a cracker!' it said in its parrot voice. 'Or maybe an Almost-Cracker.'

'You can have a cracker soon,' Dominic promised. He turned to Pearlie. 'You find the soup ladle. I'll get out the glasses.' Pearlie began dancing towards a cupboard. 'Hey!' warned Dominic. 'I've told you once already. *No dancing!* Only *almost*-dancing! This is an *Almost*-Party, and . . .'

At that exact moment the kitchen rang with a loud knocking sound. The first guests had arrived. Pearlie and Carlo ran to open the front door.

There was quite a crowd on the veranda. Carlo could recognize their green-haired bus drivers, but there were other people too, probably bus drivers they hadn't had a chance to meet as yet. In between all those heads of green hair, he could make out the blue bus, with still more people getting out.

'Come in! Come in!' called Dominic. 'Welcome to everyone.'

'Lovely to see you!' called Jessica.

'*Pop my fizzle and fizzle my pop!*' sang the Almost-Popplefizz mixture out in the kitchen, while the Almost-Parrots rose in a colourful flight, and perched on the newcomers just as if they had known them for many years.

'Ah!' said one driver, the one with the little antlers, 'I can tell where you do *your* shopping.'

'There's nothing like the song of Almost-

Popplefizz,' said the beautiful driver with the long green hair. 'There's nothing as exciting as Almost-Popplefizz — except for Almost-Fizzlepop, of course. Almost-Popplefizz is almost like the finest champagne.'

'Only much better!' said the antlered one. 'There's much more fizz and pop.'

'That's exactly what we want,' Pearlie told him. 'We can't have an actual party because that man on the other side of the hedge complains about noise, and with him being a policeman we've got to be very careful. We can't have too much popping. But we can probably get away with an *Almost*-Party, which is what we're having.'

'Have a piece of Almost-Cake,' Jessica cried. She held one of the great brown roses out to the drivers, and they each took a petal. The strange thing was that immediately new petals started to grow in place of the old ones. Carlo looked at Pearlie, and Pearlie nodded. They closed in on the brown rose and each took a petal for themselves.

The petals tasted delicious, not quite like cake, but almost like cake. They tasted rather like Christmas pudding — well, almost like Christmas pudding — and when you had eaten one petal you immediately wanted another, particularly if you'd had to share the first petal with some hungry parrot — or Almost-Parrot.

There was another knock at the door. Dominic opened it and in came a crowd of people, led by Sherwood Arden, all dressed in the flowing smocks worn by the shop assistants who worked at the check-out counters of the Supermarket at the End of the World.

'*Pop my fizzle and fizzle my pop!*' sang the voices in the background, while Jessica began passing around Almost-Cake and glasses of Almost-Popplefizz.

'Is dancing allowed?' asked Sherwood Arden. 'Or would that stop it being an Almost-Party?'

Carlo and Pearlie looked at each other, uncertain what to say, but at that moment there came yet another knock at the door. Carlo and Pearlie ran to open it.

They didn't recognize the people on the other side of the door — well, not at first anyway. These people were carrying bottles of champagne and were wearing actual party clothes, patchy pink-and-purple, glittering green, and bright blue covered in sparkles.

'We've come to join your party,' cried the tallest

one — a woman Carlo felt he had seen before. But when? And where?

'It's not really a party,' said Pearlie. 'It's an Almost-Party.'

The Almost-Parrots screamed in fury — but why?

And then suddenly Carlo remembered just where he had seen this woman before, and looked anxiously down at her feet. Under her long skirt she was wearing *gumboots* — rather old gumboots, gumboots no one with good taste would wear to a party . . . or even to an *Almost*-Party. Pearlie looked down too, and Carlo and Pearlie both knew at once just who these people were, crowding in at the doorway, waiting to be invited in.

'Dowlers!' they yelled with one loud voice, and tried slamming the door shut. But the leading Dowler shoved her gumbooted hoof in over the doorway, and called back over her shoulder to her friends. 'Attack! Attack! Take prisoners!'

The gang of Dowlers attacked, heaving and shrieking, but Dominic and Jessica, along with the bus drivers and the supermarket assistants, all nimbly sprang in to help, and nobly defended the door. The tallest bus driver, leaning over Carlo and

Pearlie, pinched the leading Dowler on the nose, shouting out helpfully, 'Down with the Dowlers!'

Carlo and Pearlie, Dominic and Jessica along with their Almost-Party guests all joined in.

'Down with the Dowlers!'

'Dump those Dowlers!'

'No Dowler-doing in this house!'

The Almost-Parrots caught on quickly. 'Down with the Dowlers!' they shouted in crackling Almost-Parrot voices. The leading Dowler covered her pinched nose with one hand, screaming in agony, and kicked wildly in at them with her right foot, but this was a mistake.

Carlo and Pearlie grabbed her right-foot gumboot, one on either side, and dragged it away from her. A fearsome foot was revealed, cleft like a sheep's hoof but much bigger, and with terrible yellow claws branching off on either side. The Dowler scratched out wildly, but Pearlie seized the doormat and flung it across her claws, while Carlo, snatching up a floor rug, wrapped it under and over, so the claws and hoof-points were totally tangled up. The Dowler was quite unable to scratch anybody.

'Ha! Ha! Ha!' laughed the Almost-Parrots, circling overhead.

While this was going on, Dominic, Jessica and the supermarket assistants, along with the bus drivers, all pushed on different parts of the door, which slowly closed and then clicked shut. But of course that wasn't the end of it. Those Dowlers kept on howling and banging at the door, determined to break in.

'Give us your bus tickets!' they were screaming. 'Hand them over!'

'They want to kidnap a prisoner or two,' cried the bus driver with the little antlers. 'And then we'd probably have to buy the prisoners back with your bus tickets.'

The snakes on the head of the Gorgon bus driver all reared up, writhing and hissing at the mere thought.

'We've shut them out, but how do we get back to the supermarket?' asked Sherwood Arden. 'Listen to that horrible howling out there!'

They all listened, and at that very moment they heard a voice shouting every bit as loudly and furiously as the Dowlers. It actually sounded even louder and much more furious.

'You lot!' the voice shouted. 'What are you making a noise like that for, and at this time of night?'

'It's the man next door,' hissed Pearlie to Carlo, 'the policeman.' And she put her mouth to the keyhole and shouted, 'Help! Help!'

'Good idea!' thought Carlo. 'Policemen are supposed to help us.' And he shouted 'Help!' as well.

'Good idea!' agreed Dominic. 'Come on, Jessica! Shout loudly!'

'Help! Help!' shouted Dominic and Jessica together.

'Help! Help!' shouted every Almost-Parrot in the room.

There was a tangled noise that lasted for quite a few minutes until suddenly, in the distance, they heard a curious howling sound that rose and fell, rose and fell.

'It's a Chief Dowler!' cried Carlo, horrified. 'It must be!'

'No, it's a police car!' Pearlie told him. 'That policeman from next door must have called the police station on his mobile phone.'

Outside there was a wild shuffling, and then the sound of about two dozen gumboots racing away. Dominic let out a great sigh of relief. 'Open the door!' he said. 'I don't think there's a single Dowler left out there.'

'But what about police boots?' asked Carlo. 'There might be a Dowler disguised as a policeman.'

Pearlie, however, was already opening the door. The next-door neighbour stood there, wearing his policeman's uniform and frowning and panting. His boots looked stern but perfectly ordinary. Quickly, before he had time to complain about the noise, Dominic held out a glass of Almost-Fizzlepop. Outside they could hear the siren, now howling at their very gate. Then it stopped, and was followed by the sound of many pounding feet, rushing towards the house this time, not running away from it.

'Thank you! Thank you!' Dominic cried. 'I'm sorry we made so much noise. That violent gang was attacking us.'

The next-door-neighbour policeman had quietened down. Almost-Parrots had perched all over him and he was looking astonished, but flattered and fascinated at the same time. 'In that case I forgive you,' he said. 'These things happen.'

He looked at the drink longingly. 'Thank you, but no! We're not allowed to drink on duty.'

'But this is a very healthy drink!' Dominic said.

'We weren't having a party — just an Almost-Party when . . .'

At that moment six more policemen came barging up the steps and onto the veranda. Dominic looked at Jessica, and then swung his arms (along with the glass of Almost-Fizzlepop) wide. 'Welcome! Welcome!' he called, in case there was any doubt about it. 'We're so grateful to you officers-of-the-law. Come in, come in all of you.'

Within a moment the Almost-Party room was utterly crowded — with family members, bus drivers, supermarket assistants and now a lot of policemen as well. It was an odd mixture of Almost-Partygoers.

'This is really wonderful,' whispered Pearlie to Carlo. 'Look! The man-next-door is having some Almost-Fizzlepop after all.'

'They all are,' said Carlo. 'And they're all helping themselves to petals from the Almost-Cake.'

'Are we allowed to join in a party when we are on duty?' asked a nearby policeman, sounding unsure of himself.

'It's not a party. It's an *Almost*-Party,' Carlo told him. 'Policemen on duty are probably allowed to join in an Almost-Party.'

The policeman was immediately convinced.

His frown vanished. He smiled. He accepted a large glass of Almost-Fizzlepop and a square of Almost-Chocolate. As he tasted the Almost-Chocolate, his policeman's stern face seemed to dissolve in ecstasy. He gave a great sigh of relief and turned to the other policemen.

'Are we off duty yet?' he asked.

'Five minutes ago!' cried another policeman eagerly. 'The new team will be out there keeping things in order. Ring the station! Tell them we're held up.'

Pearlie felt Carlo pulling at her arm. She turned, and he whispered something to her . . . something she couldn't hear. He pointed to a corner of the room where there were no supermarket people, no bus drivers, no policemen, no parrots (almost or otherwise), and no parents. Snatching yet another petal from the Almost-Cake, she followed him.

'What's up?' she asked, and then took an almost-mouthful.

'Those Dowlers!' said Carlo. 'I mean we're all in here almost-but-not-quite partying, but the bus is outside, quite unprotected. Even if it's locked, I reckon the Dowlers might get into it. They could snatch it . . . drive it away from us.'

'Let's go!' hissed Pearlie, immediately setting off for the door. Carlo followed her.

'The thing is,' he was saying from behind her, 'the Dowlers have actually come into *our* part of town. They're not just lurking around the End of the World in supermarket country.'

'Right! We have to be prepared,' said Pearlie, nodding as they slid through the door and out into the garden. The bus, parked at the gate, was still and quiet, though its stars twinkled faintly in the twilight.

chapter thirteen

CARRIED AWAY

Across the lawn they went, jumping a flower bed, then through the gate, leaping across the footpath.

'Suppose it *is* locked!' Carlo wondered. But the bus wasn't locked.

'That's a bit careless,' said Pearlie.

So Pearlie and Carlo slipped into the bus. As they did so, they both heard a sound — footsteps coming around the corner, footsteps clicking along the footpath. But these were no ordinary footsteps. The sound that was coming towards them was the sharp clattering sound of hooves, mixed with the clicking of claws. It was as if a herd of wild goats and maddened ostriches was charging down the street. No doubt about it! Those Dowlers may have been driven away from the house, but they were now moving in on the bus.

'Lock the door!' whispered Pearlie.

'No key!' Carlo whispered back. 'Hide! Quickly! Hide under the seats.'

They bent down below the level of the windows and ran quickly to the back of the bus, where they ducked under the blue velvet seats. Just in time. The bus door swung open again, and about half a dozen Dowlers burst into the bus, all cackling with triumph.

'They won't be able to start it,' hissed Carlo.

'Ours! Ours at last! We'll show them!' cackled one Dowler. 'This bus must know the way to the supermarket by heart, so let's get it out on the road. The supermarket door will fling itself wide, smiling with joy, when it sees this bus rumbling towards it.'

'There won't be anyone to protect the super-market this time round,' squealed another. 'They're all over here, flirting with parrots. The supermarket is ours at last! Ours!'

'We don't have any bus keys,' said a third Dowler, doubtfully.

But a fourth Dowler voice butted in, 'We won't

need one. We've got our super-emergency-truck-and-bus-starter. Let's have a go.'

There was a clicking noise and the bus swayed, then moaned as if it were in pain.

'Try again!' cried a chorus of Dowler voices.

The bus swayed and lurched. It was being forced to start against its will. And then . . . then it gave in. It just had to. Worked on by a super-emergency-truck-and-bus-starter, it just had to start. It had no choice.

'Drive! Drive! Steer it our way!' cried the Dowler chorus. 'Ours! Ours forever!'

'With a super-emergency-truck-and-bus-starter, we are definitely in charge of the bus,' said the driver. 'We don't need a single hundred-ride bus ticket any more. We've got the actual bus! We've taken over!'

The bus roared off into the twilight.

chapter fourteen

CAUGHT AND KIDNAPPED

The Dowlers began singing a song of triumph in squeaky voices — horrible cackling voices. Carlo and Pearlie were able to whisper to one another without being heard.

'We're being kidnapped,' whispered Carlo, 'even if they don't *know* that they're kidnapping us.'

'I've sometimes thought about being kidnapped,' Pearlie murmured back. 'You know, wanting to have an adventure. But I've always thought of being rescued as well. Who's going to rescue us?'

'We'll have to rescue ourselves.' Carlo frowned to himself in the shadows under the blue velvet seats. 'But how?'

'Let's listen in to the Dowlers,' muttered Pearlie. 'We might get a clue!'

The Dowlers were so pleased with themselves they were chattering away.

'When we get in, I'm taking all the ice cream,' one was saying.

'Me? I'm making straight for the biscuits,' said another. 'The chocolate ones!'

'You'll have to collect some for me,' said a third. 'I'm going to concentrate on wrecking the whole joint.'

There was an awful Dowler cheer. Then the voices began shouting out what they were planning to do to the Supermarket at the End of the World.

'Let's pile everything into the bus and drive away with it all!'

'Tear down the shelves!'

'Smash the check-out counter and steal the money!'

'Set fire to the silly old supermarket. Burn it to ashes and then pee on them.'

'Dance, dance, dance on the debris!'

'Grind everything to gropple-grains!'

'What can we do?' Pearlie hissed desperately.

It's hard to shake your head when you're hiding under a bus seat — Carlo tried shaking his head, and immediately bruised one of his ears. And then, suddenly, he remembered something. As his mouth fell open, the Dowlers burst into violent chorus:

'Drive the bus to the supermarket, supermarket, supermarket!

Brakes on hard — it's time to park it, time to park it, time to park it!

Burst in bawling, braying, bleating! Burst in bleating, burst in bleating!

Ours will be a mark-down meeting, mark-down meeting, mark-down meeting!

Headlines HUGE in all the papers, all the papers, all the papers,

Will record our wicked capers, wicked capers, wicked capers!'

They sang it over and over again in their horrible voices.

'Hey!' Carlo muttered, digging his elbow into Pearlie's side. 'Remember the first day we went to the supermarket? There were those shelves they told us to stay clear of, the ones surrounded by a wire fence. Remember there was a notice telling customers to be careful? It had a skull and crossbones on it.'

Pearlie frowned. Then she remembered. 'Right!'

she agreed. 'Burglar-Bite! And Pirate-Pong-out! All that stuff!'

'And Horn-Hazard,' Carlo began. He stopped. 'It might just work on *them*,' he said at last. 'I mean, aren't hooves made of horn? Well, I think they might be . . . we could give it a go, and . . .'

'Oh!' breathed Pearlie. 'Nice one! We just might be able to hold them off and . . . well . . . the supermarket people won't be staying very late at our house. I mean, it was only an *Almost*-Party and . . .'

'I think it was turning into a truly actual party,' Carlo replied. 'I mean the police were joining in, and when the police join in, that pushes things on a bit . . .'

'We'll just have to take a risk,' Pearlie whispered. 'We must protect the supermarket.'

'Big headlines in all the papers, all the papers, all the papers,

Will record our wicked capers, wicked capers, wicked capers!'

The Dowlers sang on. You could tell from the way their voices were echoing that the bus was driving in between the tall grey buildings where every door was locked and every window pulled tight-shut.

And then suddenly something clamped down on Carlo's leg. A hand! A hand with claws. Something began hauling him out from under the seat. Carlo yelled. Next to him Pearlie gasped. Carlo was being taken prisoner!

'Did you think we didn't know you were there?' said a snarling voice.

Pearlie screamed.

The Dowlers had caught Carlo! And they were pinching Pearlie as well.

chapter fifteen

TAKEN PRISONER

The next half-hour was just terrible. The Dowlers tossed Carlo and Pearlie up and down the bus, threw them backwards and forwards like basketballs, flipping them up in the air as if they wanted to score goals with them. Carlo and Pearlie banged against the ceiling over and over again, and were sometimes kicked from one end of the bus to the other. The Dowlers began chanting in victorious voices:

'First we catched 'ems, then we kicked 'ems!
These two prisoners are our victims!'

At last the bus stopped. They had arrived. Once again they were outside the Supermarket at the End of the World.

chapter sixteen

VICTORY

Carlo thought the Dowlers might lock them in the bus and leave them alone, but no! Singing their song of wicked triumph, those Dowlers grabbed first Carlo, then Pearlie, by their collars, half-pushing, half-pulling them out of the bus, and aimed them towards the door of the supermarket. Two gallant supermarket guards, who had been playing a quiet game of chess, leaped to their feet, seizing their guard-swords.

'No way in for you lot!' they cried together, confronting the Dowlers bravely. But then they saw Pearlie and Carlo, who were being hoisted high, held in those sharp Dowler claws. The guards' expressions altered.

'Let us in!' cried the leading Dowler. 'Let us in or we'll scrag these kids into mere *rags* of kids, and hang all their leftover bits over the hedges around their homes.'

'Don't let them in!' shouted Carlo. 'Save the supermarket! They can't hurt us.' However, he knew this wasn't true — the Dowlers could hurt them very badly.

The guards knew this as well. They looked at one another. Then they both sighed, lowered their swords, and stood back from the supermarket door. In rushed the Dowlers, hooting and howling, dragging Carlo and Pearlie with them.

Once the Dowlers were in the supermarket they attacked the shelves, smashing things they didn't want, and grabbing up other things — things they had longed for — and dropping their stolen goods into supermarket bags that they had snatched from beside the check-out counters. Some of them grabbed hammers from the tool section, and, once the shelves were empty, those Dowlers hammered the shelves into splinters, bellowing brutally as they did so, 'Spang them to splinters! Grind them to gropple-grains!'

Some of the Dowlers grabbed up supermarket delicacies and chomped them up right then and there. Munch! Munch! Munch! Then they spat out tiny pieces on the floor. Though he was being dragged and tossed and kicked around, Carlo noticed how the spat-out pieces lay underfoot, blinking like wicked jewels.

'Gropple-grains!' he thought. 'Those must be gropple-grains!'

And then, as he peered in a mixed-up and miserable way at the gropple-grains, he half-saw words out of the corner of his eye — saw bottles and jars and cans labelled with names he half-remembered . . . Pirate-Pong-out, Burglar-Bite and . . . *Horn-Hazard*!

By some wonderful chance the Dowlers had carried him to the very place he had planned to find. And by another wonderful chance, at that very moment, the Dowler who was dragging him along flung him sideways. Carlo was able to snatch a can of Horn-Hazard spray before the Dowler grabbed him once more, swinging him up and down, shaking him until his teeth rattled.

'Horn-Hazard!' Carlo thought, even though he was being too shaken to think clearly. 'I'm sure I've read somewhere that hooves are rather like horns in some ways. It might work . . . it just *might* . . .'

And as the Dowler, still shrieking with evil joy,

pushed him against a shelf full of tins, sending them spinning in all directions, Carlo doubled himself over the snatched-up can and struggled with the top of the Horn-Hazard spray.

'It might . . . it just might work on . . .' he went on thinking. The Dowler grabbed him again, tipping him upside down, preparing to bang his head on the floor, but, even as he did, Carlo pressed the spray lever and sprayed the Dowler's split hooves with Horn-Hazard.

The Dowler took a single step forward and then — then a terrible screeching began . . . no longer a triumphant screeching, but a screech of fear and fury, for the Dowler's hooves began steaming and dissolving. He didn't let go of Carlo immediately, and Carlo had the chance, swinging right and left, to spray the hooves of Dowlers on either side of him. One of these was the Dowler who was charging along with Pearlie just as if he was planning to score a goal with her. This Dowler's hooves began steaming and dissolving as well.

They were suddenly overwhelmed by thick, billowing clouds of steam, and a strange, smouldering scent came out of the tormented air around them. The sprayed Dowlers screamed with useless fury. Screaming and steaming! Steaming and screaming! Then they began leaping in a curious, high-stepping way. They were dancing with despair.

'Spray you to scrottle-scraps!' shouted Carlo triumphantly, for there was no doubt those Dowlers he had sprayed, along with their frightened friends, were in retreat — slow limping retreat too, because by now many of them *were* limping, their hooves dissolving into mere pegs. No Dowler could balance on pegs and they certainly couldn't run. A few Dowlers hesitated, overcome with bewilderment. This gave Carlo and Pearlie a chance to dive in among them, armed with their trusty spray cans of Horn-Hazard.

'I *thought* it might work on hooves as well as horns!' yelled Carlo, spraying the Dowlers with all his might.

'You were right! Good on you!' Pearlie shouted back.

The Dowlers were in definite retreat. 'Let's get out! Get out!' they were bawling. 'Get out of my way!' they wailed at one another, pushing their friends over as they tottered wildly towards the door of the supermarket.

'The bus!' shouted Pearlie. 'Let's protect the bus!'

By now it was easy for the children to push their

way through those hobbling Dowlers. Easy to race on past the check-out counters and through the supermarket door! The bus was waiting for them, its door wide open.

Carlo and Pearlie leaped onto its steps holding their spray cans like six-shooters, aiming them at the leading Dowlers staggering out through that supermarket door. The Dowlers took one look at them and stumbled wildly, left and right, into the shadows at the End of the World. There was a lot of howling, as the Dowler-Howlers tumbled right over the edge of the world, their voices growing suddenly fainter and fainter, dying away into thin moaning cries and strange echoes.

'We'll never come back to this wretched super-market!' yelled one Dowler. 'We'll find another one when our hooves grow again.'

'*If* they grow again!' cried another.

'We're turning into mere limping shoplifters,' moaned a third.

'We might have to limp along forever!' whined a fourth.

And, within minutes, those last limping Dowlers were vanishing, one by one, as darkness swallowed them. Carlo and Pearlie had utterly defeated them.

They suddenly felt tired. That's the thing about adventures — they can really wear you out.

'How are we going to get home?' Pearlie asked. 'Can *we* drive this bus?'

'We'll have to try,' Carlo said. 'Mind you, I think it knows the way once it's turned on, but it might need someone to steer it . . . just to make it feel secure. I'll have a go.'

'You haven't got a driving licence,' protested Pearlie.

'But *I* have,' said a new voice, and there, standing on the bottom step, was a stranger . . . and a stranger they half-recognized, even though they had never seen him before. He had green hair, just like watercress.

There was no doubt about it. There, beside them, was an actual End-of-the-World bus driver, just when they needed one. 'My alarm went off,' he told them, 'and I came as quickly as I could, even though it was my day off. But by the time I got here, you'd already saved the supermarket and the bus as well. What heroes you are! You've earned enough free Exploding Porridge and Almost-Chocolate to last you a year. And new bus tickets too, when your own tickets run out. It's going to be ages before you two need to pass your bus tickets on.' He looked around him. 'But why is the supermarket so deserted? Where are the guards?'

'Here!' said yet another voice. 'We just *had* to let those Dowlers in. They had taken these poor children prisoner and were threatening to grind them to gropple-grains. But, after all, these brave, bright kids were much too much for them.'

'We never dreamed Horn-Hazard spray might work on hooves as well as horns,' said the second guard. 'It just shows how clever kids can be, when they think sideways. The supermarket is totally saved.'

'Lock the door and get into the bus with us,' Carlo told them. 'We'll go home. If we're quick, we'll be able to join everyone at the Almost-Party.'

Anyone could tell the guards loved the idea of any sort of party, even an almost-one. They raced to lock the supermarket door with a huge silver key, then tumbled over one another, scrambling into the bus, just as the driver with the green watercress hair was settling down behind the wheel.

'Off we all go!' the driver said. 'You can sing if you like! After all, thanks to these children, we have something to celebrate.'

chapter seventeen

HEROES COME HOME

So there they were, Carlo and Pearlie, gliding along in that wonderful bus once more . . . dusty and a bit bruised by their Dowler-adventure, but triumphant.

'We did it,' Carlo said. 'We saved the supermarket.' He sounded as if he could hardly believe it, and had to keep reminding himself over and over again.

'There might be a few leftover Dowlers,' said Pearlie, 'but it will take them a while to get themselves back in order, won't it?'

'It will indeed,' said the bus driver. 'You certainly transformed their feet. Dowlers into Howlers, and no mistake!'

'Hobbling Howlers!' said one of the guards, nodding his head. 'Forget swords and guns! From now on we'll arm ourselves with cans of Horn-Hazard.'

The bus seemed to rock as it drove along — but not in any frightening way. It rocked just slightly, as if it were some sort of comforting cradle, moving forward all the time, taking them back to the city — carrying them home. They left the grey buildings behind, and came into those streets where houses had big lawns, noble old trees and flowering gardens around them — Pearlie's part of the city.

And at last Pearlie's foresty street came into sight. It was very late by now but the whole street was alight and shining. The trees on either side of the road were reflecting the glow, and waving their branches in time to the music that was overflowing from Pearlie's house and filling the night air.

'Gee!' Carlo said. 'I think the Almost-Party has turned into an actual party after all.'

Every house in the street had its lights on, but at the end of the street Pearlie's house shone out like a wild jewel. Music leaped over the veranda rail, and ran joyfully across the grass, welcoming them home, while, out on the lawn, all sorts of people danced and clinked glasses bubbling with Almost-

Fizzlepop — or maybe Almost-Popplefizz. The bus slowed down . . . slower . . . slower . . . and then it stopped.

The bus driver turned as Carlo and Pearlie made for the open door, both excited of course, but a little bit anxious as well — just what had Dominic and Jessica been up to without two reliable kids to keep an eye on them?

'That's not an Almost-Party!' Carlo was muttering. 'That's a really, truly actual party, Almost-Fizzlepop and all!'

'You're invited!' Pearlie said to the driver, quite sure that any driver of that blue bus covered with golden stars would be totally welcome. Anyone with hair like watercress was a natural guest.

So Carlo and Pearlie burst out of the bus, with the bus driver and the guards following them at a more dignified trot. Then they burst through the gate and out onto the lawn, which was all lit up and alive with dancing guests.

'More bursting!' Pearlie cried in a commanding voice, so they burst up the veranda steps, burst through the open door and burst into the crowded room. There was Dominic — Dominic dancing! There was Jessica — Jessica jiving! But sometimes it was hard to tell where one left off and the other began, because, though they spun this way and that, they always spun together again, hugging one another as they spun. Carlo and Pearlie stopped their bursting in, and slid to a sudden stop.

'You know what this means?' Carlo hissed.

'Yes,' said Pearlie. 'Do you mind?'

Carlo found he didn't mind at all. He and Jessica could probably move out of that brown flat and into Pearlie's handsome house. It certainly seemed as if there would be plenty of room for two more people. Besides, he knew he would never have another friend like Pearlie. Sharing the Supermarket at the End of the World had somehow made them close companions forever. And perhaps, somewhere along the line, he would be able to take his old friend Harding to the Supermarket at the End of the World. Or perhaps not! Perhaps Pearlie was the only friend he needed. After all, when the Supermarket had welcomed him in, it had certainly welcomed her in too. Well, only time would tell.

'I think it's great,' he said.

At that moment Jessica, looking just a little beyond her dancing Dominic, saw them.

'Kids!' she called. 'Dominic and I are going to get married. Come here and help us celebrate.'

Pearlie and Carlo wound their way through the

156

crowd of neighbours, bus drivers, policemen and supermarket assistants. People cheered them and patted their backs as they went by.

'Mum! We beat the Dowlers!' shouted Carlo. '*We* did! Just Pearlie and me!'

'We saved the supermarket!' shouted Pearlie. 'And we rescued the bus! We sprayed the Dowlers' feet with Horn-Hazard spray and it *worked*.'

There was a moment of dead silence . . . then Almost-Parrot voices squawked with glee.

'They really saved us!' someone cried. It was their watercress bus driver who had followed them across the lawn.

'They were so *clever*!' cried two voices together — the guards, of course. 'Brave as well!'

A huge cheer rose up from the crowd. The Almost-Parrots squawked again, sounding more like real parrots than almost ones. Trumpets rang out as Dominic hugged first Pearlie and then Carlo, and Jessica hugged first Carlo and then Pearlie. Then Dominic and Jessica hugged one another again. They were so good at it you could tell they must have been practising.

'Mind you, the Dowlers' feet might grow again,' Carlo said. 'They might be back some time soon. We'll have to be always ready for them.'

'They *might* be back,' said one of the guards, 'but not *soon*. It'll take ages and ages for their hooves to grow back.'

'Ages and ages!' cried the bus drivers and supermarket assistants, and even the neighbours and police, all nodding at one another.

'Carlo!' cried Pearlie. 'Didn't you hear? They're getting married — your mum and my dad! You're going to be my brother.' She looked up at Jessica. 'And can I be your bridesmaid? I've always wanted to be a bridesmaid.'

'Our supermarket sells wonderful dresses for brides and bridesmaids,' said a supermarket girl. 'All sizes! All colours! You can try them all on, and have the ones you like best for free.'

'Free's just wonderful!' Jessica exclaimed.

'I can be your best man,' Carlo shouted to Dominic.

'We've got best-man clothes too,' said another supermarket voice. 'And we can help you celebrate. We can throw another party, like this one. We're good at throwing things! Always hit what we aim at.'

There were cheers from everyone including the neighbours and police, who were obviously having a wonderful time and were already looking forward to being invited to the next party, almost or otherwise.

'I'll order in a lot more Almost-Fizzlepop!' cried yet another supermarket person. 'Cases of it! And Almost-Popplefizz.'

'And I'll reserve the other bus — the green bus with daisies,' said a bus driver in an excited voice. 'It hasn't been used for months. Poor thing! It needs to get out on the street again.'

Carlo snatched yet another petal of Almost-Cake from a passing dish. Who can tell about life, he thought. One moment I was in a brownish flat, feeling tired in a saddish way . . . the next I was having adventures at that Supermarket at the End of the World . . . and now, here I am, eating a petal of Almost-Cake and . . . and I've got a new sister to dance with if I want to. And I *do* want to. It just shows how important it is to catch the right bus at the right time.

Dominic and Jessica were already dancing again. Carlo took Pearlie's hand and they spun like wild tops, laughing and snatching bits of Almost-Cake, dancing their own dance, while the whole strange world, supermarkets and all, danced and spun along with them.